WHO STOLE STONE· HENGE?

By the same author
Murder After Tea-Time

M

e.1

WHO STOLE
STONE·
HENGE?
Leela Cutter

ST. MARTIN'S PRESS
New York

Design by Angelica Design Group, Ltd.

Library of Congress Cataloging in Publication Data

Cutter, Leela.
  Who stole Stonehenge?

  I. Title.
PS3553.U86W48 1983 813'.54   83-9701
ISBN 0-312-87043-4

First Edition

10 9 8 7 6 5 4 3 2 1

To Claude & Virginia, with love and appreciation

WHO STOLE STONE·HENGE?

1

IT WAS A TRUE MONSTER, nourished by Arctic ice, unimpeded by the frozen expanse of tundra above the Great Circle; it roared across the open North Sea, freezing shut the Kattegat, feeding voraciously off the moist ocean air as it tore into Scotland. Stone and heather posed no barrier; laden with snow, wind, and an almost palpable sense of malice, the blizzard descended upon England's heart.

Despite the howling gale, Mr. and Mrs. Battleboro were snug as two bugs. Smug, too, about their insulation from the cruel elements raging outside. Their isolation from the storm was more than just the natural insularity of middle-class horizons; although that might have been a contributing factor. Their coziness was assured by the keen foresight of Mr. Battleboro and a loan from the bank for home improvements. Tight storm windows had been fitted, and every crack and joint caulked against the most determined zephyr.

This evening, being a Wednesday, was going to be a special treat for them; their favourite show was just coming on the telly. The Missus had prepared a light snack of potted meat on biscuits, accompanied by a wedge of Stilton. She hurried to place everything on her new tin tray commemorating, with lurid illustrations, the royal progeny. Everything arranged, she entered the living room in time to hear the last thematic notes of Elgar's dirgelike Concerto #1. It was safe to clatter the dishes a bit as the solemn announcer, an expatriate American writer, condensed the previous episodes. The screen darkened, and Part Four of *The Plague Years* began: "The Deadly Mite."

In a few moments they were nearly as engrossed in the spectacle as in their snack. "Ugly great sore, that," the Mister mused as he masticated a mouthful of Spam.

"And it was the fleas! Imagine! I always thought it was the rats," she remarked, eyes fixed on the gloomy scene: wet cobblestones; black moss growing up the sides of the glistening stone walls of the narrow alley; a heap of clothes, still containing a body, huddled lifelessly before a locked doorstep. A rat, looking oddly clean, walked neatly by, eye fixed on some point just offscreen, as if a handler with a piece of chocolate were directing it to come. The tube darkened into an interruption that was altogether too long.

"Blasted Jap set!" the Mister groused, licking crumbs from his moustache.

"Best give it a tap, dear. Crikey! Look at that!" The picture had returned—in a manner of speaking. A pulsing ball of light rolled down from the top of the screen, disappearing at the bottom. It was a globe of yellow surrounded by a blue halo. With an electric snap from its innards a series of lines radiated across the screen, pulsing and chasing each other like abstract bolts of lightning gamboling on a midsummer day. The Mister rose, annoyed by the pyrotechnics, bent on finding out what happened to the skinny little bloke that had run away to the monastery. He gave the set a firm blow with his fist, after being careful to first remove the photos of various family members that rested on top. The fireworks continued unabated. He brought his hand down again with more passion this time. In response the set exploded, a great bang and flash of sparks blowing off the back cover as black smoke rolled out, smelling of burnt plastic. "Bloody blasted Japs!"

Only a few miles away in Amesbury young Bobby Fulham was twirling the dials, RFing across the wavebands, hoping to tune in one of the American stations that broadcasted on shortwave from Germany. None of the BBC stuff: Punk retrospectives when Punk was as passé as nappy pins when disposable diapers came in. No thank you, not for this lad. Trust Old Granny BBC to finally latch onto New Wave about a year after it had washed out to sea! Next thing you knew, they'd stumble across Reggae. But those army boys, homesick for the States, got a steady diet of the *real* music of the eighties. Bobby put his cowboy boots up on the bed and leaned back, one hand on the tuning dial, his eye resting on his "Dukes of Hazzard" poster.

But no joy—all he could pull in was a strange static that seemed to be getting louder. He changed wavebands. The noise, a curious chirp, counterpointed by a heavy rattling beat, did not go away, it was growing louder. He turned down the volume—

or tried; the knob was too hot. He scrambled under the table for the plug, yanking it out of the wall socket. The noise died down. He could smell hot insulation wafting from the grillwork of the radio. The smell of money burning up, he thought bitterly.

Taffy Mathin did not have an electronic device to pick up the strange happenings in the stormy heart of darkness. His own senses were filtered through an alcoholic haze behind which he had spent the better part of the evening barricading himself. It kept him warm despite the snow driven about him by the wind that whipped at the Burberry pulled over his ears. Janet—lovely Janet—who had glowed like a golden angel from across the booth—had gone to fetch the car, which was only a few doors down in a local garage. She had been going on and on about never making it home; but he had only laughed. It was taking her a long time. Growing impatient, he wandered out for a "wee bit of fresh air" that was so fresh it threatened to inundate him, bury him in one of the soft drifts, which didn't seem like such a bad idea—they looked as white and cozy as down. He staggered towards them, drawn by their pristine beauty. As soon as the bright overhead coachlight was no longer beside him, he became aware of another, considerably more remote source of illumination. He turned his face up to the wet flakes, smiling into their soggy kisses as he gazed at the whirling heavens. There seemed to be a purplish glow out over the Plain, a blob that generated a waving blue-red corona over the horizon line of council flats across the street. It seemed to pulse, as if an aureole were falling to earth. Even in his stuporific condition, he knew it wasn't possible for anything to glow through the heavy snowfall from behind the houses twenty yards away, let alone out on the high chalk plains. It could only be an optical illusion. Or worse, the drink! A man who only drank two nights a week shouldn't be experiencing delirium tremens so early in life. Appalled by the implications, a frightened Taffy retreated to the relative shelter of the welcoming pool of light from the pub.

Taffy's vision was corroborated afterwards by several sober eyewitnesses, including a motoring constable who had been stuck in a snow drift, and whose radio had acted in an intolerable fashion. The constable, having served in the army in Berlin, was convinced it sounded like somebody was trying to jam his radio. As he walked back to the station, he too saw the strange lights—not just over Salisbury Plain to the north, but over his head as well. A conscientious man, he hesitated to report this phenomena; it might be just a concomitant of a storm of unparalleled ferocity, or perhaps the aurora borealis somehow blazing through.

When he arrived at the stationhouse, he found that making a statement was unnecessary. There had already been reports—dozens of reports of unusual disturbances. In the next twelve hours of the storm the calls continued. The telephone was the only means of communication for an area of some six square miles from Salisbury town extending up the river past Amesbury and on to the unsettled Salisbury Plain itself.

The roads were impassable, and radio and televi-

5

sion received nothing but what the newspapers came to call the "Interstellar Heartbeat"—the electronic counterpart of the storm's howling nimbus. For some the isolation was frightening; they couldn't fathom what could be causing these weird events—or worse, they could! The constabulary was overwhelmed. As imagination triumphed, eyes were reported glowing outside latched windows. But were the windows latched? Too late to check! And the door to the garden—that scratching and banging! As in earlier centuries, hooved prints were sighted in the snow; Old Nick himself seemed afoot. All this during the period when visibility was nil and no one actually dared go outside for fear of becoming hopelessly lost; the perfect conditions for the birth of rumour and fear.

But Old Nick was the bogeyman of a simpler century. Alien invaders quickly replaced the devil, growing in stature with each mysterious click on the line or sudden loss of connection. There were reports of ships in the sky, of the radio speaking in strange tongues. Those who dared lift a curtain could clearly see the extraterrestrial light show. It lasted nearly to dawn before finally fading away.

John David Hilsebeck came by his cynicism naturally as the cross-pollinated progeny of a Welsh music-hall dancer and an Australian bush pilot-cum-philosopher. A childhood spent flying around the world had left him with an indecipherably faint Aussie accent, a tremendous vocabulary for describing disaster, and an unflagging conviction that the world could go to hell in a handbasket—as soon as he was out of it.

Pragmatically and philosophically the present position he occupied suited him right down to his instep; and while his grousing disguised it, he was a happy man, having found his niche. His feet were up on the desk as he slouched back in a swivel chair that, by some miracle, did not dump him on the paper-littered floor. It was not much of a cubicle, this Night Desk; but since John David was asleep, it did not bother him.

The phone on the desk rang; it was just past 5:00 A.M. In the windowless closet there was no hint of the storm's grudging abatement outside. With the skill of one who had served in the military, Hilsebeck attained complete consciousness by the third ring. "Night Desk," he said, sounding perfectly alert, another trick he'd learned, along with listening in his sleep.

"Snoggin' away, are we?" A curmudgeon's voice on the other end of the line.

"Jenks," he replied, stifling a yawn.

"*Mister* Jenks, you young cur."

"And what cheery word have we got this morning, Mein Führer? Bit early, isn't it, for Your Editorship?"

"Now that we have the pleasantries out of the way, I need a story covered. Much as it grieves my heart, you are the only one who can do it."

"Time you recognised true genius."

"Pah! You couldn't construct a grammatical sentence if your job depended on it. And damn it, it does! Now I have no doubt it's going to be a blasted cock up—"

"No news is bad news."

". . . due to the blankets of snow that even now

7

smother the byways of our picturesque little shire. To wit, the roads are closed and you are the only staff on the spot to handle the story."

"'Killer Storm Strafes Salisbury.' Not since Luftwaffe bombers roared over fair England's—"

"Not the storm, you lout! The UFOs!"

"Aliens here in England's pastures green? Saints preserve us! Have they looked up the queen's knickers?"

Jenks held his breath long enough to convey exasperation, though in truth, he relished Hilsebeck's sauce. The old blusterer had been managing editor since the year dot, and the owner for the past two centuries. The Salisbury *Plain Speaker* was strictly small beer, and he had years ago given up fancying himself as a reincarnated Beaverbrook. "All the old ladies—of both sexes—spent the night on the phone working themselves into a dither. I suppose it's due to misdirected hormones, but a spook, nonetheless. All the tellies and radios went out, even the police bands," Jenks said.

"Could it be the military's doing?"

"I don't know, I suppose it could be those mysterious outsiders who drive around in unmarked military vehicles, but it wouldn't be our local army boys—they mooch about in old jeeps and take their tanks over jumps, reliving El Alamein. The biggest news they ever produce is a bent wing on a staff car, especially if they follow true to Colonel Bellows' form. He's the security head—and the man to see if it's general beating around the bush you want. Had the devil of a time dealing with the old fool during that series we did on army wives: 'They Also Serve.'"

Hilsebeck groaned into the receiver. "I researched part of the piece."

"Ah, you're familiar with Bellows, then. At any rate, he's still their front man; first in war, first in dissimilitude."

"I'll tear him into little bits."

"Just so—but he's one of those inflatable toys—knock him down and he bobs back upright. Otherwise, I can think of little else to brief you on, proper pushing lad that—"

"Deserves another ten quid a week."

"Can easily be replaced," Jenks countered smoothly. "But quickly, lad! Mustn't let the London dailies beat us on our own turf! Go to it, man!"

But the London dailies were already on their way while Hilsebeck was slogging ineffectually along in his snowboots. It was not much of a race. On the *Plain Speaker*'s side, there was the matter of distance; the office in which the temporary night editor had been sleeping was in the heart of Amesbury, less than a third of a mile from police HQ. But the main street was hip-deep in snow, slow going even for Hilsebeck, a tall man with a slightly rawboned look who seemed capable of simply exploding through the light powder. His appearance was deceiving: on a Melbourne beach he could pass for a second-string lifeguard, yet he was lazy and detested any strenuous form of exercise. Like any sane person, Hilsebeck took advantage of the benefits that broad shoulders, neat moustache, hazel eyes could bring, but he put no effort into his appearance. His clothes were inevitably cheap and off-the-peg, his hair unkempt and a little too long. And he wasn't the sort who would notice a fresh spill of cigarette ash on his lapel, or a sleeve soaked in the puddle of some pub's countertop. He enjoyed his vices, abhorred serious work, and had enough brains to avoid it. He considered himself, in rare moments of introspection, a genial sort of slob.

As such, he did not exactly race down the white furlong that lay between him and what was the logical place to start—the local constabulary. The sky was still leaden, an overcast that reduced the ceiling to about a thousand feet, according to his practised aviator's eye. (He'd logged some two thousand hours of flight time at his father's side flying deliveries, dusting crops, and spotting lost sheep in the Queensland outback.) His galoshes were filling with snow and threatening to slip from his feet with each flailing lunge; he had to push himself ahead like a snowplow. Rounded hillocks were everywhere, the burial mounds of the automobiles that had been abandoned during the storm. Huffing and cursing, he hoped no one had left a bicycle on the road; if he tripped and went down there wasn't a St. Bernard for miles.

A muted roar from behind brought him to a halt. He felt snow coldly creeping up his trouser legs as he turned to see a dark shape overhead—a helicopter. Must have cost a pretty packet, he thought as it clattered above him, its rotors insolently creating an instantaneous storm that engulfed the reporter, blowing off his scarf as the whirlwind continued down the avenue and hovered over the park. Although he hadn't seen the markings clearly, he had a good guess who it was. Only one thing could excite him from his usual torpor, and that was the possibility of putting it to the Big Boys. And a whole load of the sacred cows were now disembarking from the helicopter that had landed near the statue of Romney. The city press had arrived. With the distaste of one who had once been a member of the elite J.D. Hilsebeck loosened his metaphoric gun in its holster and prepared to come out spitting lead. Old Jenks knew his man: this was one situation that got him going. The competition had just gotten into the first curve ahead of him, but he wasn't out of the hunt by any means. He would lay back and watch the hairier lads shunt each other off into the muck.

He could hear their voices inside the police station as he wrestled off his galoshes in the foyer; his shoes and socks had gotten soaked, his feet felt numb to the bone. It was going to be a long, uncomfortable day.

The doors from the foyer into the main waiting room of the police station were the swinging type. It was like a saloon scene in a Western as he pushed through and stood momentarily, the doors swinging back and forth behind him. There was the inevitable fleeting hitch in conversation as the faces turned to stare.

J.D. recognised a few from Fleet Street, seen once or twice in bars, or on the sidewalk talking and belching after an expense account lunch. And, inevitably, Devereux—the man who had replaced him after his "extended leave" had stretched out into nothing at all.

Satisfied that he was one of their tribe—something about the smirk on his lips, or his gimlet eye must have marked him—they returned to their restless talk, thinking aloud as they kept watch on the two doors that stood to either side of the duty constable's desk. A balding red-faced veteran of some twenty years was busy talking into several telephones simultaneously. He and the journalists ignored each other: when the door opened and the chief constable appeared, then their work would begin. Until that moment, they contented themselves with idle chatter concerning perks and gossip and complaints. What kind of per diem did the scandal sheets give? How far was *The Times* in Queer Street? Was there a decent hotel in this backwater?

"Mornin' Hilsebeck." Devereux detached himself from the others who had flown in with him. He was a slightly wilted carnation, a bit past the first flower. A medium-sized man who looked smaller with his sloped shoulders and perennially lowered eyelids, beneath which lurked characterless orbs. The slightly drooping corners of the mouth, and pronounced lines running from them up towards his nose, gave him the appearance of being rundown, over the hill. In fact, he was a year younger than Hilsebeck's thirty-five, and had the reputation for being every editor's dream. Hilsebeck held no grudge just because he had been replaced by him, nor resentment against the paper itself. The monolith had found J.D. too sporadic in producing the sort of dreck that sold papers. "Speculative, too original, better suited to the literary world," his severance notice had said, and Hilsebeck agreed. Problem was the literary world involved far too much work and far too little cash.

"You boys after flying teacups?" Hilsebeck casu-

12

ally inquired. "Perhaps the Lady or the Tiger?" He nodded towards the two doors that were the focus of attention.

Devereux turned the corners of his mouth down a little further, which was the expression he tried to pass off as a familiarity. "Knocked up in the middle of the night, shunted off to the helipad, just to cool my snow-soaked heels in a smelly little office. A devil of a way to make a living."

Hilsebeck lifted one lip in a sneer: true he held no brief against the man for replacing him—he just hated him for his grotty little self. The self-deprecation was just so much bilge. Beneath those sparsely scattered hairs—it always looked like it had just rained on Devereux's head—lurked the brain of a weasel. The meek facade was just a good way to lower the victim's guard, then in with the meat hooks. High calibre, my arse, Hilsebeck thought, and not for the first time. He'd read some of the man's stuff: the sort of knifework that just skirted the edge of a civil suit. If newspaper reporting—not a calling Hilsebeck had ever considered particularly honourable—was slipping into a new generation of muckraking and cheap pandering, then it was being ably assisted by the likes of Devereux and his cronies in this room.

Well, it would be interesting to see how Chief Constable Coggs would deal with these outsiders; none of them had bent the elbow with the old bull like Hilsebeck. There should be a few exclusive tips—not for direct attribution, of course—for the local representative of the area's largest newspaper. There bloody well had better be, or no more buying rounds for the chief at the local pub. But what was keeping him?

The chief's main preoccupation, at that very moment, lay at the other end of the wire. The receiver, held in one meaty paw, had brought its tales of terror all through the long, hard night. Coggs had consumed no less than fifteen cups of tea as well as most of a flat-sided bottle marked "Danish Liniment" that he kept in the bottom drawer of his desk. And at this hour the man felt as empty as that impromptu flask, which made it heavy going trying to understand what this silly ass Nordstromson was gassing about. Calling from a public box—to judge from the sound of it. The Swede's phony loverboy accent didn't aid matters at all.

"Try to get hold of yourself, man! . . . Yes, yes, I understand how you got there. You skied—well then?" he demanded impatiently. It wasn't like this frosty foreigner to sound so excited. He cupped his forehead with his free hand and listened to the torrent of absurdity pouring into his ear. Comprehension slowly dawned. "Missing? Of course I believe you know what it looks like! It's on every bloody postcard in town, isn't it!" Coggs let his entire body droop forwards onto his elbows propped on the desktop. He still held the phone, but he was no longer listening. He thought he'd heard everything in the past twenty-four hours. But all that airy-fairy nonsense was cool logic compared to this! No, no, it was too absurd to credit . . . but *if* it was true it was the crime of the century! Even bigger than the Great Train Robbery, and there'd been tons of publicity about that one—even a book and a movie, hadn't there?

14

2

GUNNAR NORDSTROMSON was a product of his own reputation. He had arrived in Little Puddleton for a year's sabbatical from the University of Stockholm, and his status as Don Juan was firmly established within a few weeks of his arrival. Perhaps his first affair with the notoriously loose-lipped barmaid at the Blue Man Inn had facilitated the speedy dissemination of the Swede's vital statistics. Certainly Doris was not one to keep her opinions to herself. At any rate, Gunnar's notoriety as "that randy Viking" soon became a fixture of gossip in all of Little Puddleton's environs.

Nordstromson accepted the responsibilities of his position with good grace and a great deal of energy. He had plenty of free time since his academic work required little besides extended walking tours and a bit of mapping. For an archaeologist specializing in pre-Roman Britain, the location was ideal: with the ruins at Woodhenge, Stonehenge, the chalky downs of Hertfordshire, and the splendid assortment of burial mounds that dotted the area, an archaeologist could not fail to find ample grounds for study. He travelled as he pleased, a rucksack on his broad back, his long, thick legs showcased by walking shorts most of the year. He gained a first-hand knowledge of the out-of-the-way spots that were perfect for a refreshing break from a long hike, whether alone or with one of the local beauties. Sometimes several of them, it was rumoured.

As one who made it his business to keep a finger on the town's pulse, Chief Coggs had special reason to notice the fluttering hearts left in the "scandal-navian's" wake. The chief could do nothing but be rude to the outsider and make certain his own daughter, Tricia, was kept under stern parental control.

Little Puddleton, Nordstromson's home base, was a mere village. The thatched houses, picturesque inns, Norman church, and the melodious flow of the nearby canal attracted the weekending, coun-try-home set from London, as well as summer tour-ists. Even the name was perfect, thanks to some long forgotten Victorian who had descended upon the valley, rechristening everything in sight with a variation on the River Piddle. Lower Piddlecross-ing, Piddlebridge, etcetera, became Puddle this and Puddle that, in order to confer a greater dignity on the locale. As far as the local populace was con-cerned, it hardly mattered, since the story of the name change was now one of the popular anec-dotes told to countless amused visitors.

Today Nordstromson and Tricia Coggs had de-cided to take advantage of the storm to effect an escape. The extraordinarily heavy snowfall, fol-lowed by crystalline clear air were perfect condi-tions for cross-country skiing, unobstructed by fences, traffic, or Tricia's father. The chief was not only snowbound, but inundated with work. The

Swede had a particularly interesting place in mind, a location both convenient and resonant with mythic implications. He packed a thermal blanket and a bottle of wine into his rucksack and they were away.

He forged smoothly ahead, his powerful legs bulging rhythmically as he surged forwards, blazing twin trails in the loose powder. Close behind, Tricia glided along in the slick runways plowed by the Nordic giant, all the while studying the way his muscles rippled underneath his tight blue nylon plus fours and form-fitting red jersey. These Swedes definitely knew how to dress to their best advantage. She barely noticed the gently rolling hills made more beautiful by the fresh snow. Fences, roads, and signposts were buried under a gleaming white blanket. Gunnar maintained a brisk pace with complete navigational confidence: after all, he'd been over this turf countless times, viewed it from the air, memorized topographic maps. He'd brought along his map and compass purely out of habit.

Atop the curve of a hill he leaned abruptly and came to a stop. Steam poured off his body, as if he were on fire, a thrilling image that compelled Tricia to slip her arms around his waist and press against him—which wasn't easy without tangling skis. And Gunnar wasn't cooperating. Instead he was staring aloofly off towards the distance, a perplexed frown clouding his classic features.

"Give us a kiss," she pleaded, but to no avail.

"It isn't there!" he muttered, disengaging himself and launching down the hill in a cloud of powder like an Olympic competitor in sight of the finish line.

"Wait! Where are you going?" she shouted after the rapidly receding figure. What was this in aid of? A new game? If so, it was too athletic for her tastes. By the time she caught him she would be too winded to have the strength to wrestle. She pursed her lips, let out a few disgusted sighs and dug her poles in to push off. He was well ahead, but stopped after a mile or two, messing about with his compass and map as she came puffing up. He lined up the red vernier line on the transparent plastic and muttered to himself, glancing up at the sky in bewilderment, then consulting the map again.

"This is not my idea of—" she began, but he cut her off with a babble of Swedish. "Please speak English!" she ordered, feeling her temper getting the better of her. It was one thing to be a fascinating foreigner, but there was no excuse to start acting peculiar and lapsing into that rude guttural.

"Are you *blind,* woman?" he shouted, waving his arms wildly in front of him. "It's gone, don't you see?" The terrible expression on his normally placid face alarmed her.

"What are you talking about?" she demanded.

He didn't answer, only turned and pushed off again. She hung back, considering her options. It might be clever just to head back to town—but how far was that? She looked round, slightly panicky, wishing she'd been paying more attention to landmarks—but there weren't any! Of course, she could follow him; it was the easiest option, though not completely to her liking. Who knew what a Swede gone loopy might do? Mum had always said she didn't trust anyone with pale blue eyes. A bit of fun was one thing, but being scared quite another. She vacillated for a moment, then set her jaw and swept down the hill, joining him at the edge of a depression where he was stamping his skis, compacting the snow.

"The tunnel must be right here," he was muttering, too intent to even look up at her.

"What—agghhh!" She screamed, as the snow suddenly gave way beneath her and she fell into a dark hole. The landing was hard—thank heaven for the padding of long underwear and polyester-stuffed ski gear! Gunnar slipped down the small avalanche she had created, calling, "Are you all right?"

"I think so."

"Good! Do you have a coin?"

"A coin!" Her shrill response echoed the length of the concrete tube. "What the bloody hell for?"

"For the telephone." He pointed at the instrument hanging on the wall beside them.

Her eye caught the mysterious writing on the wall: SUE LOVES BOBBY, PUNK SUCKS, NUKE THE IRA. Then she knew where she was. She pulled a moist piece of paper from her hair—a shredded bit of brochure covered with lurid letters: VISIT STONEHENGE. Comprehension hit like a ton of bricks—so that was why he was going on queer! For a moment she thought she was going to be sick.

"Hil-se-beck," Devereux drawled, elongating each syllable, pronouncing it with punctilious courtesy. John David silently noted that this little twit had polished up his BBC accent since his ascendancy to blue-eyed boyhood. If this was preparatory to some future career change—say, in the direction of a television news desk—it would take considerably more skill than Devereux possessed to put strength into that recessive chin and twinkling bonhomie into those googley eyes. "Old man, I wonder if I could have a word," he intoned in his casual cocktail party manner. The desk sergeant had once again waved aside their impatient demands to see the chief, and the rest of the imported talent had bunched up. Hilsebeck had not joined the move to storm the chief's sanctum sanctorum, despite his intimate status as drinking buddy. At times like this the chief would either hole up like a badger or charge about like a berserk musk-ox. If the second condition should occur, then as local reporter he should have a distinct advantage over these interlopers. Until then, he would be available for Devereux's crudely predictable approaches; for the moment rapprochement seemed the order of the day.

"Sit," Hilsebeck replied, clearing a space as Devereux separated himself from the huddled group of newsmen.

"Thanks very much." Devereux sat down with every sign of exhaustion. "I say, J.D., how did you come to be so Johnny-on-the-spot? It's shocking out there; a chopper is the only hope, I'd say. . . . You fly, don't you?" he added parenthetically.

"Like a bird." He let the putdown slide right by. Devereux not only knew he'd walked, but walked from an insignificant newspaper with only regional circulation. "By the way, where'd your pilot wander off to? We could swap a few tales to pass the time," J.D. said. Mutual aviator skills seemed to produce a great deal more camaraderie than the wary chumminess of Fleet Street.

The other man sighed, pinched the bridge of his nose, and rubbed his eyes as if scrubbing out the last grains of interrupted sleep. "I have no idea. Gawd, what an assignment. I hadn't expected to be covering anything like bug-eyed monster stories." He didn't have to add: after I got your job. "All these . . . phenomena! I'm sure there are the usual logical explanations: electrical discharges, lost weather balloons, mass hysteria. . . ."

"Weather balloons?"

Devereux frowned. He hated to be made light of. "Figuratively speaking. Most, if not all, such reports are nothing more than misinterpretations of readily explainable events. For instance, the tracks of Old Nick leading up to the neighbour's porch—patently the work of an overzealous religious imagination directed against an unfriendly neighbour."

Hilsebeck considered this for a moment, his eyes wandering aimlessly around the waiting room as he responded, "I saw a UFO once. It gave me the jim jams."

"Oh go on."

"I was in a biplane over the Bush, just at twilight. Saw a gaseous ring, bright pink and pulsating rhythmically like so." He panted loudly a few times. The other reporters, standing in a closed circle like yaks in a gale, turned in unison to gape.

Devereux coloured slightly. "You needn't pull my leg."

"Now why would I want to pull your leg, old man?"

The rhetorical question hung in the air as the chief's door flew open with a bang, and Coggs himself, in a wild apoplexy, emerged on the dead run. Or at least at the top speed his massive bulk allowed. He gave the appearance of great forces unleashed as he plowed into the group of reporters trying to encircle him and bring him to a standstill. Like a water buffalo shrugging off so many bothersome dik-diks, Hilsebeck noted.

Coggs was shouting at his sergeant, who had shot up from behind the desk, dropping the phone in mid-conversation. "My coat, you damned fool! Get a car ready! Come on man!"

The confused underling sputtered, "But—the roads are impassable, sir!"

Coggs scowled at them all, reserving a special glare for Hilsebeck, who was still lolling on his bench. "Who are these idiots?" Coggs demanded of his aide-de-camp.

"Newsmen, sir."

"Good morning, Chief Constable, I'm from the—" Devereux endeavoured to gain his attention, but was brusquely interrupted.

"And how did they all get here? Dog sled?" His voice dripped scorn as he fought his way into a mammoth overcoat.

"Helicopter, sir," came the sergeant's reply as he handed him the official peaked cap. "Parked outside."

Coggs' piggy eyes lit up. "Then we shall commandeer it." He pushed past the journalists, who were squawking in protest. "What do you mean, I can't! Consult your Articles of Incorporation: 'Any authorized police officer . . .'"

Devereux was forced to acknowledge a point well taken. "We are more than willing to allow you to expropriate our helicopter. However, we expect to accompany you, and there is the problem of available space." They could all recognize the smell of a story, and each intended to be in at the kill.

No bucolic policeman was going to escape their clutches without a fight.

"Where's the pilot? Not drunk, is he?"

"Not at all; an excellent fellow. But it will take a moment to locate him." Devereux smiled, hanging onto his position as group spokesman.

"Then get on it!"

"Ah. . . " Devereux paused meaningfully. "This raises a delicate problem. When we arrived every seat was filled. It will be necessary to leave one man behind. . . ." He was drowned out by a chorus of heated objections from his fellows. "A lottery would be fair," he shouted above them.

Coggs shook his head. "I need two seats. I have to have my sergeant." He sucked in his breath, trying to remain calm. Just another moment of this irritating delay—no point in bursting a blood vessel. "I suggest you get a move on and locate your wandering pilot. You may sacrifice two of your number in any way you fancy. Sergeant, give him a pistol for that purpose." The sergeant dumbly reached for his hip gun, then blinked, and caught the joke. "Look nippy! You've got five minutes!" Coggs bellowed.

Loudly bickering among themselves, the reporters funnelled out the door. The chief rolled his eyes, then snapped orders at his man. "I want a camera—the instant print kind. Local topo maps. And fill a thermos with tea . . . eh?" He paused, caught the drift of the man's grimacing, and turned around. "Hilsebeck! Why don't you scurry off with the rest of the jackals?"

"No need," was the nonchalant response. "You know, Coggs, I've got six hundred hours in type."

"What type?"

He nodded over his shoulder. "That ship sitting out on the green. We used 'em for aerial spraying."

The chief was anything but slow off the mark. "Get that equipment, Sergeant, on the double!" Then he turned back to the reporter, admiration twitching the corners of his lips. "J.D., you are a cad! Won't your colleagues cut up rough?"

"Not if we avoid them."

"Having them all for a mug! It's dirty, but I'm in a rush." He slapped J.D. on the back. "This just might work out to our mutual advantage, my boy."

"I gather this is something fancy?"

"You have no idea! It could be the making of both of us!"

They made quick tracks to the helicopter, the sergeant following, juggling an armload of paraphernalia. It was a piece of cake—not even an ignition key to worry about. Hilsebeck buckled into the harness, flipped on the master power switch, and in a few moments the turbine was vibrating to life. The rising whine brought the London boys on the run, floundering through drifts, shouting. As Hilsebeck lifted off he noticed one figure in an anorak and visored cap who was shaking his fist in the air. Apparently they had located the pilot—but only a moment too late.

"Where to?" he threw over his shoulder.

"The intersection of the A303 and A344," came the reply from the back cabin.

"North by west?"

"Right. We're going to Stonehenge."

"No problem," he replied. Then he lowered his voice before adding, "By the way, I don't have a license to fly this bird." As he intended, they couldn't hear him above the steady beat of the rotors. Formalities satisfied, Hilsebeck directed their nose towards The Story of the Century.

The air was clear and the slight impressions of buried highways made navigation less difficult. To make it easier, J.D. followed the main road west out of Amesbury, navigating as would any carborne tourist. But he became confused upon approaching the intersection: Stonehenge should have been just back in the angle formed by the two roads, but there was nothing there. "Afraid I got lost somehow!" he shouted back to Coggs, who came forwards and leaned between the front seats, peering at the empty expanse below. "I can't fathom it—it ought to be right here. . . " He swallowed the rest of the sentence. He had just noticed several concentric circles of evenly spaced depressions. At the center of the innermost circle was a ring of much larger depressions. "Good God!"

"Bloody unbelievable!" the chief cried. "Take some pictures, Sam!"

"I don't understand," Hilsebeck mumbled, for once thoroughly stunned. He slowly circled as they scanned the surface. The snow was completely unblemished except for two delicate sets of ski tracks. "No sign of heavy equipment. Just a ski trail! No sign of the fence . . . there's a hole where the tunnel must be . . . this is impossible! The damned things weigh fifty tons!"

"Behold the work of extraterrestrials—the very same bastards who made all the funny lights last night and mucked with everyone's gogglebox. The same who tapped on Mrs. Simmons' front door and made the dog howl." The policeman's voice was sarcastic.

"Either the work of Martians or the Russians—it'll be the work of one or the other." J.D. smirked. "Even though you and I and our fellow skeptics will chuckle at the balleyhoo, it will sell a million papers. And Chief Constable Coggs shall become a household word." Letting the cop chew this one over, the reporter set the auto pilot and took some shots with his own 35mm. The chief made no objection, too intent on fantasies of fame and promotion—maybe even a chat show appearance.

"There's someone down there," the sergeant called. "Just to the left there. Signalling."

"That's the Swede. I told him to stand by. Put us down, J.D."

"Look at those trails—two sets in together, then a single set back out."

"I noticed. It's clear the randy ferret brought one of his dollies out here for a romp on the altar, then sent her off before we could catch them at it. What some cheap tarts will do!" The chief shook his head, but with less heat than such brazen carrying on usually inspired.

They created a mini-blizzard setting the helicopter down on the car park. The Swede, despite his height, resisted the common impulse to duck away from the churning blades. "A cool one," Hilsebeck thought, switching everything off.

They jumped down, sinking to their waists, thrashing awkwardly towards the relative comfort of the pedestrian tunnel that led under the highway to the monument's site. As they stamped the sticky snow from their feet, Coggs eyed the Swede with undisguised disgust. "And what brought you out here, Nordstromson?"

"My work."

"Your work!" The chief snorted. "Nice work if you can get it, eh?"

"I suggest we confine ourselves to the urgent matter at hand. If you require my assistance, that is."

"Of course, you can be our expert on the scene. I'll make a few calls and you can give us the guided tour." He sloshed towards the phone, concealing the inner turmoil that suddenly gripped his insides. Who to call? His immediate district superior? Scotland Yard? They were notorious publicity hogs, and he wasn't about to share the limelight with anybody. But what choice did he have? He could claim his calls to his senior officer didn't get through due to the storm, leaving him no choice but to go right to the top. After all, this was what amounted to a national emergency. But how did one get through to the Prime Minister? He only had a few pence in his pocket, and he'd be damned if he'd ask his companions for spare coins. Every movement from now on must be calculated to look well in print. A terrible self-consciousness overtook him, but didn't weaken his resolve. No, he wouldn't share this gem with anybody, at least not without a fight. He dropped a coin in the slot and waited for the operator to come on the line. It would just have to be collect.

3

"This is the limit! Just too much to ask of a body, enough to make a decent person up and walk off the job!" These were Phyllis' bitter thoughts as she dragged the ladder out of the basement and propped it against the kitchen wall. The frightened terrier was yapping from under the shelter of the sideboard, while the lady of the house stood by dithering apologies about all the egg on the ceiling. She went on and on, but Phyllis would let none of it penetrate her silent sulk. None of it made a bit of sense anyway. The old girl was really going off her onion. A danger to herself and the community. It was a shame, but there it was.

"Oh Phyllis! Will you leave off the dramatics! I didn't do it just to annoy you. It was a matter of scientific research," Lettie Winterbottom said.

This last bit was enough to make Phyllis break her stony silence to grumble righteously, "Didn't I warn you about that contraption the day you brought it into the house? There's no telling that we aren't mutated already. I've felt a pain in my left eye from the moment you had it installed."

"Now don't be absurd. The pain is only your sinuses acting up again, and you know it."

"On Monday I felt like I couldn't wake up all day long. That was right after you turned that infernal thing on!" She pointed with a sponge dripping bleach towards the machine, then resumed scrubbing at the ceiling.

"Pure hypochondria! Nothing to do with my experiments! I was already aware that an unshelled raw egg will explode in a microwave oven, of course, but that wasn't enough information, don't you see? How far would it blow the door off? And with what kind of force? Enough to kill someone? And would two or three eggs be more explosive? And where would my victim have to be located if I were going to snuff him this way? Sitting at the breakfast nook having a cup of tea? There were so many vital questions that I—"

"There isn't another housekeeper in St. Martin's who has to clean egg off the ceiling, is all I know," Phylis growled.

"I'll make it up to you. Take the rest of the day off," Lettie offered contritely, and when this didn't affect the glower on her daily help's horsey face, added, "With pay."

As was her way, Phyllis didn't respond immediately, but carefully considered the offer, and how she should take it. If she left early it would be letting the old Bath bun off too easily. Better to stay all afternoon and wash the drapes, making a show of her righteous indignation. Tonight she would call the niece and tell her in no uncertain terms how Lettie was deteriorating. Something had to be done about it.

The housekeeper's call brought Julia Carlisle to St. Martin's that weekend. The drive from London was slower than usual, but at least the roads were clear of snow. Julia knew that Phyllis was a bit of a gawd-help-us and didn't expect to find her aunt "greatly deteriorated," as the housekeeper had described her. Still, Lettie was a little scatty at the best of times, and it wouldn't do not to look in on her.

"What's all this about eggs?" Julia inquired when their affectionate greetings were done with and the ebullient Tim was shoved down off her new woolen trousers.

"Trust Phyllis to make a fuss! It's nothing un-usual, I'm just betwixt and between again. You know how that always goes. I'm so distracted by my search for a new idea that—"

"I noticed some fresh dents in your Humber. Phyllis said you'd been smashing into a variety of things."

"That cheeky tattle! See if I don't give her a good wigging!"

"Well, what about it?"

Lettie fluttered her hands and blushed, but still managed to make it sound perfectly understand-able. "I was nipping along on my way to Upper Wibblestone when suddenly I noticed a piece of lint on my sleeve. I was removing it when somehow I banged into a stone fence. I have no idea how it could have happened."

"And what about the bash on the other wing?"

"That time I was taking Tim for a little outing.

You know how he loves to go along and bark at everything. It gives him so much pleasure that I don't like to scold. . . . Well, we'd just turned the corner on High Street when he spotted the postman and tried to leap out the window after him. I was so startled that, what with one thing and another, I smashed into the Vicar's saloon, which was parked in front of the ironmonger's."

Julia shook her head, giving the dog a disgusted look that he mistook for an invitation to get back in her lap. When she put him firmly on the floor again he growled and went off to chew on her luggage handles. "Auntie, I think it would be wise to use a cab. I hate to think of you injuring yourself—or someone else."

"Now, it's nothing so serious! Just a little spell of writer's distraction. I will be perfectly all right once I settle down to starting a new one. Don't you remember all those mishaps I had between *The Corpse Took Two Lumps* and *Lambs and Lemmings*? I even wound up with a broken ankle, but it was well worth it because I met that wonderful young surgeon who told me about dermatographia, which was the very idea I needed for a new plot."

Julia winced—it hadn't been one of her favourite gimmicks, seriously marring, in her opinion, the plot of *Lambs and Lemmings*. Dermatographia is a hypersensitive skin condition causing the tissues to release large amounts of histamine in response to trivial stimuli. So, the lightest stroke on the skin produces a red weal, making it possible actually to write on the skin. Since countless murder victims had already left clues written in sand, ink, blood, dust, and gravy, Lettie thought it would be a catchy

31

idea to have one write a clue on his own skin. Apparently sales had been high among medical professionals—hundreds were given away as door prizes at the annual symposium for dermatologists held in Glasgow.

"That's all well and good, but the point is you ought to take precautions when you know you're distracted. You ought not to drive—"

"But I am too distracted to notice that I'm distracted. And before I know it, I'm crunching into a snow bank."

Julia's normally wide, lovely eyes narrowed to angry slits. "Wait now! You didn't go out driving in the snow!"

"It was only just a few flakes when I left to go to the decorator's."

"The decorators! What was so urgent that couldn't wait until the roads were safe?"

"My bedrooms, of course! You know I'm redoing each in a different flower motif. And when the shop called to say the lilac paper was finally in, I was so excited that I had to rush right out and see it!"

"I know what this recent frenzy of decorating is all about—and I don't approve," was Julia's worried pronouncement. It had developed, though her aunt would never admit it, into an obsession. Although the two had never met, Lettie had resented Gwenna Hardcastle for forty years. Gwenna Hardcastle, the queen of historical romances, and Lettie's nemesis. As if her fame, her millions, her face-lift weren't enough for Lettie to have to read about everywhere, just recently Gwenna had been asked by an American linen manufacturer to de-

32

sign a line of their sheets and towels. When Lettie heard about it, she had paled. What did that sex-fixated old snob know about interior design? Lettie dropped broad hints to her publisher, and was re-doing her cottage in the pathetically unfounded hope that some magazine would want to feature her obvious good taste in an article on homes of famous authors—thus giving the world a chance to see that Lettie knew more about colour and texture and knickknacks than Hardcastle ever would. All of this struck Julia as a distinctly unhealthy preoc-cupation for a sixty-year-old lady: it could only lead to bitterness, and was unbecoming to an otherwise sweet old pet. Julia had often said as much, but got no satisfaction or promises of mended ways. Lettie would always tell her she was exaggerating and drift off into a description of Tim's recent digestive problems, which made it impossible for him to keep anything down but boiled chicken breast and minced steak. "I honestly believe he's developed an allergy to tinned horse meat."

Knowing when she was licked, Julia changed the subject. "Have you been following the news lately?"

"Not for days. You know I don't keep in touch when I'm like this."

"Then you haven't heard about Stonehenge?"

"Of course I have! I've visited it several times and once used it as a nice background for *The Stuff Screams Are Made Of*. Surely you can't have forgot-ten the scene where the murderer stalks his victim among the stones only to—"

"No, no—the *latest* about Stonehenge. It's miss-ing."

"Missing what?"

"It's vanished. Stolen. Or sent back in time. One headline reads 'Souvenir Hunters From Outer Space—Reclaiming Their Own Or Intergalactic Vandals?' Need I say the press is going bonkers with it?"

Lettie dropped her knitting, her clear blue eyes glazed over in wild glee. "Stonehenge stolen! Isn't that wonderful!" She sighed, clapping her tiny blue-veined hands together. "Any clues?"

"The papers say nothing as yet. The whole area is heavily guarded, but the police can't clear the snow for fear of disturbing what evidence may be underneath."

"No signs of big machines?"

"Not in the snow. No one can be sure how it was managed, or why. Wildly spectacular, but a pointless crime."

"No, I wouldn't think pointless. . . ."

"Anyway, I brought you some clippings, just in case you'd been out of touch. And I knew it would be just the thing to amuse you."

Lettie fell on the articles eagerly, automatically dividing them into two piles. It was easy to differentiate just by reading the headlines: the pulps leaned heavily on the outer-space angle, suggesting everything and anything, with no facts behind any of it, except some hardly credible witnesses claiming to have seen multilimbed creatures cracking whips over a team of robot moving men. The voice of reason, on the other hand, seemed only capable of ineffectual sputtering. Apparently there had been enough phenomena—at the moment unexplained—to make the UFO angle attractive; there was precious little to support any saner theory.

Even *The Times* spent an inordinate amount of space debunking patently ridiculous scenarios that hardly deserved acknowledgement: giant dirigibles, fleets of helicopters, etcetera.

Lettie laughed out loud at the science fiction stories and only glanced at the copiously illustrated sidebars that detailed Stonehenge's original construction, ancient uses, remaining mysteries. With these she was already familiar, having researched Stonehenge history for years.

"Remarkable, simply. . ." Words once again failed her. She lapsed into a prim little smile, looking like she must be dreaming of girlhood memories or planning what kind of buns to bake for the church bazaar. But Julia knew what that angelic look really meant and patted her hand. The dangerous period betwixt and between would surely be over now.

"This one fellow who was in at the discovery seems to have a head on his shoulders. Some local writer, by his byline, but syndicated to most of the nationals. I'd say he is unquestionably the man on the scene. Why don't you give him a tinkle and introduce yourself?"

Lettie shook her head. "No need, I've met him before. Very straightforward young man, not English at all. . . ." She paused, giving her pretty young relative a shrewd, Victorian look. "You'd find him interesting."

But Julia only shrugged. She was off men lately, still licking her wounds from the last unhappy ending. Her aunt always tried to draw her out about these sort of things, but Julia never wanted to talk about them, feeling uncomfortable trying to translate modern relationships into the old-fashioned fluff the old dear still believed in. "So, you've already got a few ideas about Stonehenge, do you?"

"Oh yes . . . I understand part of it, but there are a few vital questions that remain."

"Auntie! You've only read some clippings!"

"True, dear. But since I happen to be a dab hand at the background, I am one step ahead."

4

THE PAST FORTY-EIGHT HOURS had been heavy going for John David Hilsebeck; the amount of energy he'd been expending was exorbitant, especially for one who valued his leisure. He had a crying need for some rest, but the whirlwind that had caught him up showed no signs of slackening. At least a position at the eye of the storm gave him an unparalleled view of events. He could only tough it out and, like Coggs, milk it for all it was worth.

The chief constable's initial attempt at self-aggrandisement had been a painful disaster, from which Amesbury's head minion of law and order had not yet recovered. He had managed to reach the PM's personal secretary in a short time. But this worthy had taken only a few moments to tick off the chief, producing a flush that had rapidly suffused from his blue serge collar upwards to the broad expanse of shiny forehead. Wasn't it patently obvious that the Prime Minister's office was not the appropriate level to contact, the secretary had curtly inquired. His police superiors were not available? Then that would be the military's province, wouldn't it—treat it as a disaster. As a final insult, the secretary had informed him that the PM's office would contact the local army unit while Coggs stood fast and waited. Security for the operation would be temporarily the chief's responsibility. Not a word must leak out until precautions were taken. The secretary brusquely hung up, without mentioning what precautions or why. Probably the PM needed to trump up a good alibi before the media got to her. She'd doubtless clandestinely sold Stonehenge to the Arabs in order to foot the bill for another year of misgovernment.

The injunction to establish the D-notice came too late; even as the chief sweated through his call, Hilsebeck was making for the helicopter. He climbed into the pilot's seat, ostensibly to warm himself in the sun's feeble glow that was filtering through the broad windows of the flight cabin. In reality, he was removing the long scarf that he'd casually wadded between the front seats before they'd taken off from Amesbury. He'd done this to protect the copter's radio telephone—his contact with the newsdesk. Coggs hadn't noticed the device, obviously not aware that there was one on board.

It was one of the latest units, making it possible to dial direct rather than having to wait for the special operator that was still required on older models. He did not dare get caught, and every second was valuable. Jenks answered the first ring. In ninety seconds, J. D. delivered the message, as well as getting assurances that all articles would be under his byline as reporter on the scene. He also gave permission to sell the scoop to a major wire service and accepted Jenks' offer of 60 percent of any outside income. Jenks was smart enough not to waste time haggling over percentages. Only when they were ringing off did any note of excitement creep into the conversation. "Put your back into it, sonny boy!" Jenks cheered. J. D. hung up and hid the phone again; it was vital to keep it secret as long as possible.

The army's response was quick and zealous. A fleet of helicopters flying in tight formation swarmed in to land, disgorging heavily armed troopers all over the area. Coggs ran around waving his arms and shouting impotently as the louts trampled all over his evidence. In a matter of minutes the pristine surface was obliterated under heavy boots and the impressions of over-eager bodies that had spread-eagled themselves in the snow, weapons ready.

Hilsebeck leaned against his purloined craft, composing his own version of the debacle, using built-in censors to make the scene palatable for the readership. In these declining days of the empire, editors wanted verbs that cracked whips, Up British in flavour—nothing anti-military to spoil the game of heroes. He took some quick snaps, then surreptitiously removed the film cassette and inserted a fresh one—he knew the military mind too well. The Swede, observing the scene with growing bemusement, nodded conspiratorially at J.D.'s sleight of hand. The reporter made a mental note to chat him up as soon as the opportunity arose.

The ground troops signalled in the mother ship, a considerably larger copter that landed and disgorged the brass. Among them Hilsebeck recognised Colonel Bellows. From the shoulder patches and unit badges, it looked like most of these lads were from the security division. This wasn't surprising, quite a bit of secret work was done there. There was probably even a Special Intelligence Service man along to monitor the army.

The officers kept in a group, ignoring the four civilians who were obviously slated for Bellows' personal brand of disinformation. As Bellows, a round teddy bear with overblown moustache, approached, Coggs made an effort to regain his temper. He must try to avoid blowing off at the colonel just because his bleedin' soldiers had trampled all over valuable evidence.

"Morning, gentlemen. Coggs, I presume?" He nodded in the direction of the right uniform, and the chief constable took another deep breath and introduced his sergeant, then Hilsebeck. "Oh yes," Bellows gave the reporter a raised eyebrow. "I've met this man." He then focused a gimlet eye on the Swede.

"And this is Nordstromson," Coggs explained.

"So good to see you again, Colonel," the archaeologist politely murmured.

"Mr. Nordstromson reported the—" Coggs began, to cover a palpable tension between the Swede and the colonel.

"Right," Bellows interrupted, which was part of his style—never allow anyone to finish a sentence of more than five words. "Now, Hilsebeck—never forget a face, you know. Or an unkind account. You caused quite a flap with your article about that missin'—reputedly missin'—Kraut Leopard II tank that we borrowed."

"Long live NATO," the reporter replied, unable to resist.

Bellows considered some proper form of revenge, momentarily settling on a threatening glare. He then turned sharply to survey the field of battle and address Coggs, who was now just behind him. "Let's have the facts."

Coggs rolled his eyes heavenwards and delivered a to-the-point summary in only slightly hostile tones. If he had to associate closely with this ass, he'd better stock up on a couple more fifths to replenish the Danish liniment bottle.

"Damned fine work, Constable. Everything tightly under wraps; that's the best way to keep it. Be glad you got the military here in time before the damned Third Estate got in here mucking up the scene with their cameras and tape recorders."

"Fourth," J. D. interjected.

"Eh?"

"We're the Fourth Estate."

"Well jolly good for you. Is that suspicious lump in your coat a camera, by any chance?"

"It is."

"You'll have to hand it over. No, not to me. One of my officers will take care of it presently."

"Doubtless." Another staring contest was avoided as the sound of still more rotor blades became audible, coming out of the east.

"Curious, we didn't bring in any choppers from that way," the colonel muttered. In a short time it was overhead, a solid blue job, with loudspeaker dangling under its nose. Inside they could clearly discern another sort of uniform: dark suits, striped ties, trench coats. "Civilians!" Bellows cried in disgust.

"Not quite." Coggs smiled, savouring his revenge. "Scotland Yard. *My* boys."

"But how . . ."

"The lines cleared just after I called the PM," the chief lied sanguinely. "I have channels too." Once he knew the army was on their way, he hadn't hesitated to call his own superior. The more hawks tearing at the carcass the better. He hoped they would distract each other long enough for him to recover lost ground. He had no intention of being the official whipping boy. Situations of this magnitude had a nasty way of producing a goat.

"Well, you might have told me." The colonel was also aware of how the buck could get passed down the ranks. Colonels, like chief constables, were at about the right rank to make a good sacrifice.

The initial encounter had set the tone for the internecine bickering between the military and the police. Coggs, while not yet disgraced, hardly stood in high regard with his higher-ups for letting the army get there first to bung things up. A compromise had been eventually reached whereby the military got exclusive control of both entrance and exit from the scene. Inside the khaki circle the police began to investigate, greatly hampered by the near-freezing temperatures. As civilians, Hilsebeck and Nordstromson were allowed to leave as soon as they swore to say nothing to anybody until contacted by one of Bellows' lackeys. They confiscated J.D.'s camera, read him an abridged Official Secrets Act, and let him go without forcing him to take the pledge. He was well away from there, nursing a much-needed glass of Guinness, when the story broke.

It was a publisher's dream come true. Jenks had the first edition of the *Plain Speaker* on the streets by one o'clock that afternoon, a full two hours ahead of the London dailies. The story flew far and fleet, distributed by the international wire services. Within hours it was being broadcast around the globe.

As days passed and no new developments could be reported, the media focused on Hilsebeck himself. He made good ink—what other handsome if sloppy reporter could fly a jet helicopter, get the story of the century, then break it before the heavy lid of secrecy could fall? It was as neat a job of reporting—not to mention nose-tweaking of the authorities—as had occurred in many a moon. Even Devereux and the others he had so efficiently skunked, were compelled grudgingly to contribute copy to his nascent legend.

But to the bureaucrats, the army in particular, he was now the enemy. He had evaded them; worse, he had done it legally by acting before they had enjoined him to silence. Once the story was out there was little they could do to suppress the furor of interest. Secrecy can't thrive for long under the strong glare of publicity. Until they could somehow get the goods on him, the authorities would have to vent their collective spleen by freezing him out of any further information. Their attitude was enthusiastically shared by Coggs, who moodily ejected him from the station. It was going to take all of

J.D.'s inventiveness to glean any more information from any official source.

Hilsebeck was back in his cubby hole resting and plotting. Despite his ascension to reportorial godhood, there was no place more commodious to put him. But at least someone had been impressed into service as his secretary, handling the constantly ringing phone, winnowing the chaff from the grain. J.D. was very much in demand, to the point where fatigue had left his eyes permanently half-closed as he leaned back in his chair, feet once more firmly planted on the desk.

Jenks swept into the tiny office, wispy white hair askew, grey eyes bright behind tiny wire-rimmed spectacles. "When would you like the fatted calf served?"

"Hold the calf. Make it a couple of vestal virgins."

"Maudie down in printing may be available. Her mandatory retirement isn't until next month." He dropped a pile of fresh newsprint, still wet. "Feast your eyes on these." It was the first run of the afternoon's special edition. The enormous banner read: STONEHENGE—EXCLUSIVE PHOTOS.

He squinted at the highly abstract looking black and whites. "Nice clear reproduction—you can't see anything," J.D. pointed out.

"Nothing but snow. That's why I've got the pictures below the fold. The banner will suck them in. But what's your next move? Got anything up your sleeve?" The old man sat on the edge of the desk, as time-honoured a pose as the younger man's sprawl.

"Just writer's cramp up to the elbow."

"Maybe this Swede will pan out."

"Maybe. If we get really desperate we can always do a four-part serial on him, cataloguing his multifarious sexual conquests. It will all tie into Stonehenge, since that's what brought him to the scene on the fateful morn. We could sell it to the big scandal sheets. Then all the sex mags will be after him to pose starko for their centerfolds."

"Don't come that bored tone with me."

"All veins of gold must come to an end eventually. I'm only trying to prepare our naked egos for the letdown."

The editor groaned. "Spare me the rationalisations. If you let up now, you're a bigger ass than I ever dreamed."

"Only an ass would presume to solve this whole loopy affair against the combined wrath of the army, CID, police, and the Royal House of Windsor. I'm not Sherlock Holmes."

"Oh stuff a sock in it and read what just came in on the wire." He shoved a bit of paper in J.D.'s face, forcing him to take it. "It's from that American weekly that's forever being sued."

"Bum fodder." Hilsebeck grimaced.

"Just read it!"

Hilsebeck obeyed, eyes slowly widening, all desire to sleep vanishing as he whistled elatedly. "Two hundred and fifty thousand dollars!"

"Just a tiny bit sweeter than the paltry five thousand pounds this country's papers could muster! And all you have to do is locate the stones so that they can be properly identified."

"For two hundred and fifty, I'll carve up a new set."

"Someone will try, I'll wager. Think of it! A quarter of a million!"

"But our own beloved Inland Revenue will try to take eighty-five percent. Fortunately I know a good tax man." Shrugging hurriedly into his coat, John David cried, "I'm off."

"To see the Swede?"

"I'll have to postpone that interview. I've got a more important expert to see."

"Who?"

"All in good time. By the way, what does it take to find a tax haven?"

"Just a lot of bloody cheek, and a ticket to the Bahamas."

"Then I'm in." The journalist nearly ran out of the office, a new energy in his shuffling gait. He just had time to get to the library. Now what was that barmy old crumpet's name? Riverbottom?

5

JULIA WAS ALONE in the house, puttering around in the kitchen, repotting some African violets into lavender and rose-coloured pots, recent purchases of Lettie's in keeping with the new decorating motif. Her aunt was out taking Tim for a run. Julia had just gotten her hands covered with soil when she heard a knock at the front door. That was odd, most of Lettie's village friends tapped lightly at the back. Julia washed her hands and went through the living room, wondering if it was a salesman.

She opened the door and beheld a man's back as he was returning to a shabby red car that could just be seen above the snow that hid the picket fence. There was no sign of a Hoover or a briefcase bulging with magazines, so she called out, "Hullo."

He turned around, a good-looking specimen, though bleary-eyed. His tweed coat was rumpled, a multicoloured scarf draped unevenly around his neck. He squinted around a cigarette like a pack-a-day man. "Hullo yourself. I nearly broke your door down."

"Yes, just like a rabid bagman."

"But now that you see me, you know I can't be—

I'm not smarmy enough." He lapsed into a pitchy voice: "Fancy a colour television on the never never, just five bob a month and no need to make the first payment until next Whitsuntide." He grinned and looked the better for it. He sauntered towards her, as if it were too much effort to lift his feet. "The name's John David Hilsebeck."

She told him her name and asked what he wanted, if he wasn't selling anything. He produced a press card. "Is the old girl about?"

"Meaning my aunt? Oh! You're the man from Stonehenge! *Do* come in!" Her sudden switch from polite forbearance to positive effusion took him slightly aback as he wiped his feet and followed her inside. "Let's go into the kitchen, it's the only room that the decorators aren't in the process of disrupting." She gestured at the mess of tools piled in one corner of the living room. All the furniture was pushed to one side and covered with plastic to protect it from paint. The workers would return in force on Monday.

Hilsebeck stretched out his long frame in the breakfast nook, taking in his surroundings and hostess with a practised eye. "Okay if I smoke?"

"Lettie doesn't approve."

"Oh well, I'll just hold it in my mouth unlit then—that will stave off the nicotine fit for a while. Is there any hope of a cup of coffee? I never could learn to like tea. Just boil me some coffee in an old tin can and I'll be happy."

"Is that an American custom?"

"Probably. I acquired it in Australia, though. My taste for a Kahlua chaser did come from America."

"I see. Well, Auntie has never heard of Kahlua,

but I think she does have a coffee machine here somewhere that she once received as a gift. . . ." A search through the cupboards unearthed a complicated German device that was filled with sweets. "Doesn't look like she's ever used it." Julia dumped the candy into a dish and assembled the pieces. "We were both impressed with your articles. They seem to be everywhere."

"Yeah, my day in the sun."

"You don't sound very impressed."

"It's one quick step out of the top of the tree."

"I suppose you're right."

"Don't misunderstand, although I've never wanted to set the Thames on fire, I am not completely without aspirations. A warm stretch of sand, a jug of gimlets, a beach bag bulging with cash, a smiling bikini. I am as you find me—a misplaced beach bum."

"What are you going to do about it?"

In answer he produced the rumpled copy of the press release on the reward offer. Julia perused it with a deepening frown. "I won't allow you to manipulate her."

"Just because I've got a press card, doesn't mean I'm rotten to the core. My motives are unblemished—I just simply want the Yankee dollars—surely you can appreciate that? Wipe that grimace off your face, woman, or I'll swallow my cigarette in my anxiety."

"Nobody likes to see naked greed."

"No, personally I prefer it in black lace knickers and garter belt. But offensive jokes aside for the moment, this deal is as safe as a bank. I'll cut your

Auntie in for half the swag. She knows her stuff and I need a partner."

She returned his steady gaze, trying to fathom the depths, if any. Finally she relaxed and said, "Good. Lettie needs a partner too—not that she's thought of it yet."

"Dear me, John David! Such an attractive offer!" Lettie gasped. "All that money! And I suppose there will be an indecent amount of publicity."

"As indecent as you fancy; I can guarantee it." Hilsebeck looked thoroughly contented spread out on the crewel rug in front of the cheery fire. He had been well fed on kidney pie and now the warmth was lulling him to sleep. He had even persuaded the old girl to bring out some brandy. It was just about heaven, in contrast to the past few frenetic days, and he said so.

"There will have to be a contract, of course." Lettie murmured happily, eyes on her knitting. The clacking of the needles presented an agreeable accompaniment to the crack of sap from the oak log. "It shouldn't take too long to get everything all tidied up, once we agree on the particulars."

"You sound like you have it all solved," Julia remarked from her spot on the divan, wrapped in an afghan. This conference reminded her of the disjointed mutterings of three slowly recovering victims of sleeping sickness—not the most dynamic business meeting she'd ever attended, but underneath the nodding coziness the wheels were turning.

"In a way," Lettie purred. "But as to the particulars—half the reward money and a guarantee of a

50

Sunday supplement feature article with full-colour photographs of every room."

"Whatever you say." J.D. nodded, yawning and stretching.

"You're such a nice boy. Julia, dear, are you still in touch with that school chum—the one whose husband ran away with another woman so she divorced him and joined the Druids?"

"Natalie, yes I suppose I could get in touch."

"Excellent. I need to pry some sacred mysteries out of her."

"I don't expect you could. They frown on that sort of thing, I hear."

"But if you appealed to her as an old school chum. . . "

"I don't think old school chummery carries quite that much weight."

"That much weight, exactly!" Lettie mused.

"What?"

"Yes, what can—that is the question," Lettie agreed.

"Auntie, please! What can what?"

"What can carry that much weight—a million tons or so."

Hilsebeck was suddenly awake. The old girl was getting to the nitty gritty, although it still sounded like waffle. "You have a theory?"

"Oh yes." She continued placidly knitting while the two young people gawked at her in disbelief.

"Well?" they both chorused.

"All in good time. We haven't drawn up the agreement yet."

The document was duly drafted and signed, but Lettie continued to be vague, saying she had to go to the scene first and inspect a few geographic features. Hilsebeck was easy about it. No sense in badgering the old thing. Might as well have another nip of brandy. Tomorrow was another day, and it was impossible to contemplate the two-hour drive back to Amesbury tonight. When he gave voice to this reluctance Lettie readily recommended the local inn. Eventually he dragged himself off the floor and maintained a slightly wavering upright position long enough to make for the door. Julia showed him out.

On the doorstep he glanced out into the frigid night and said, "Don't send me out alone. Come have a nightcap with me at the inn."

"Thanks very much, but I think not."

"Attached?"

"No, more like detached—withdrawn from the game."

"Once burned twice shy."

"Something like that."

"What a pity." His voice and smile were redolent with invitation—"we'd be good together" they said, but he was much too clever to actually verbalize anything that trite.

"Good night."

The door closed firmly in his face.

6

THE NEXT MORNING dawned too early for Hilsebeck's tastes, but at least he had the company of
Lettie and her interesting niece to keep him awake
on the drive back to Little Puddleton. Never at his
best before noon, J.D. made a few lame attempts at
seductive charm before lapsing into a bleary silence
and devoting his attention to avoiding snow banks.
Lettie chattered away unremittingly about nothing,
eliciting an occasional amusing response from Julia.
The soft spice of Julia's perfume drifted under his
nose, making him wonder what manner of god it
would take to make this cool bird sit up and take
notice.

The answer came a few hours later when they all
met Nordstromson for lunch at The Blue Man Inn,
where Lettie and Julia planned to stay. The Swede's
first smouldering look seemed to rivet Julia to the
spot as he gripped her hand and displayed a blinding expanse of white enamel.
    Smiling knowingly, Lettie settled into a chair. To
hide his irritation J.D. stalked over to the bar and
ordered a pint. When he returned Julia had come
to her senses enough to nod vaguely at him as he

took the seat across the table. The Swede was already cosily wedged right next to her.

The bitters and the bitterness at this puerile display of poor taste on Julia's part were so distracting that J.D. was barely able to follow Lettie and Nordstromson's enthusiastic discussion of Stonehenge's mysterious history.

"Of course, the Druids had nothing to do with the building of Stonehenge. It's sadly typical that the misinformed public still believes they did." Nordstromson dismissed the majority of mankind with an impatient wave of a tanned hand, which casually came to rest on Julia's wrist.

"But," Lettie countered, "the lure of 'Earth Mysteries' will always glitter. . . . Even Monmouth's twelfth-century claim that the magician Merlin brought the stones here from Ireland by mumbling magic words—"

"Surely you don't credit such foolishness!" the Swede exclaimed.

"No, but I do appreciate its appeal. Such charming nonsense! Like the old legend that it is impossible to count the stones and get the same number twice."

"Absurd! If your forbears couldn't get the same number twice it was because they were slipshod buffoons!"

"What was that you said about our forbears?" J.D. grumbled in the testy manner traditional to conversations in pubs since time immemorial. "But kindly set me right—if it wasn't the Druids who built Stonehenge, who was it?"

"Recent evidence," the Swede began, his tongue purring over the holy words of his science, "seems to indicate that construction took place over a period of eighteen hundred years in six phases. The most significant parts were built by a group we call the Beaker people, a warrior-pastoral society that traded as far away as Greece and Ireland. The workmanship of the monument indicates that an architect may have been brought in from the eastern Mediterranean."

"Outside talent," the reporter muttered and rolled his eyes. "Bloody foreign architect, wouldn't you know?"

Lettie sighed in the general direction of her partner, who was carrying flippancy a bit too far. The Swede was making no attempt to hide his disdain for Hilsebeck's loutish behavior, smiling at Julia with manful tolerance. Lettie hoped the mild antagonism between the two wouldn't escalate. An uncomfortable silence ended when Nordstromson launched into a starchy sounding pronouncement about the possible uses of the monument. "Of course, there is a good deal of substantiation for the theory that it was used as a solar and lunar observatory. The post holes indicate lunar observations carried out over a hundred and ten years. The station stones form an accurate rectangle with two parallel sides indicating the midsummer sunrise; the other two indicate the moonrise and moonset at major standstill."

Hilsebeck commented that who the hell knew what a major standstill was, anyway. His readers wanted meat, not this meringue that the archaeologist had been serving up by the spadeful. In spite of this irreverent interruption, Nordstromson launched into yet another lecture, this one on the different kinds of stones, their source, and the methods used to transport them to the site. For the bluestones, it was a journey of some fifty miles—by primitive raft via the River Avon, then overland on large sleds and rollers pulled by hundreds of workers.

Lettie seemed to make much of this, remarking, "Isn't progress wonderful?" and intimating that whatever the ancients could do with hundreds of men over the course of several years, moderns could accomplish with just a few workers, some clever machinery, under cover of seventy-two hours of bad weather.

The Swede interpreted her observations as an indication that the military were the culprits, an idea Hilsebeck enthusiastically embraced, saying, "After all, it's their turf. Maybe one of their latest weapons—a meganeutron laser—accidentally went off and vapourised our oldest monument."

Nordstromson nodded. "The lights in the sky, the electromagnetic disturbances."

"What a story! 'Secret Weapon Goes Wrong—Stones Slagged.'"

"Stuff and nonsense!" Lettie exclaimed. "Such an idea is absurd. Although the army might have the technology required to move the stones, what possible motive would they have for taking them?" There was a lapse in the conversation as each pondered what the army would want with Stonehenge. No one came up with any ideas, so Lettie eventually continued. "The problem is that there are no warehouses nearby, nothing but open plain. Where did the thieves hide their equipment and how did they transport it during the storm? These are the keys. . . ."

J.D. was about to ask her to explain exactly what she was getting at, but clammed up, casting a blatantly suspicious scowl in the Swede's direction, which was returned with icy Nordic eyes. To prevent a scene, Lettie got up quickly, tugging at the reporter's arm and saying, "We can discuss this matter while you give me the tour of Little Puddleton."

"All right," J.D. agreed. "You'll excuse us, Nordstromson. Coming, Julia?"

Nordstromson smoothly took his cue, resting his hand possessively on her shoulder and remarking that skis were the only way to tour. Julia eagerly agreed. "It's settled, then, I'll take you out now."

J.D. heard Julia making some idiotic remark about how athletic Nordstromson must be as her aunt steered him out the door. "It's shocking the way you just left her alone with that masher," he grumbled, too snookered to notice the hypocrisy of his self-righteous anger.

"Julia can take care of herself," was Lettie's unconcerned response as they crossed the street. She stopped to look at the display in a wool shop window. "Lovely mohair! I wonder if it comes in mauve."

Her companion lit a cigarette and tried to quash a desire to stuff the wool down the impossible old nit's throat. It had been a thoroughly disgusting day thus far, and he'd had too much to drink just to laugh it off.

"I'd better be going. I need to survey the landscape below the scene of the crime in order to determine if my wild theory is even worth mentioning."

"Take the ski tour with Julia," he suggested behind an evil grin. "Gunnar would be thrilled to have you along."

"Oh, I don't expect they'll be going that way at all." Lettie chuckled, earning a befuddled gape from her partner. John David preferred his old ladies conventionally Victorian. It shocked and repulsed him to hear this one apparently blithely condoning her own niece's casual encounters. "Stop goggling at me, young man," she said sternly. "Now pay attention. I need the use of your automobile for the afternoon. Kindly give me your keys."

He obediently relinquished them. "You are beyond me, madam. But never mind. I left the car parked in front of the tea shop. If she won't start, roll her down the nearest hill."

"I shall manage, thank you. Perhaps we'd better meet at the tea shop at four to discuss developments."

"Right. If you want me before then I'll be at the newspaper office cutting out paper dollies."

The old sports coupe, between rust patches, was a dull oxidized red. She cheerfully took note of several dents—so reassuring in the event of another of those inexplicable accidents she'd been having lately. The interior bore evidence of Hilsebeck's housekeeping. The foot wells were nearly ankle deep in wadded cigarette packets. A wave of flotsam slid forward as the car lurched to life, like debris washing in with the tide. Several of last summer's tennis balls threatened to roll themselves under the pedals in an orgy of self-destruction. Lettie, whose credo was neatness in all things, had to restrain herself from pulling over and bailing the greater part of the debris into the nearest ash bin. But she mustn't presume; after all, the trash was his personal property.

The roads had been cleared, but a foot of snow

remained on the ground. As she drove up the shallow slopes to the crossroads where Stonehenge should have been, the lower areas that were dotted with trees and villages fell away. The transition was a quick one; the sterile, open contours of Salisbury Plain seemed to leap up, full-blown, in the blinking of an eye.

She stopped at the intersection, considering whether or not to proceed on to the actual site. From here she could see two army vehicles parked a few hundred feet up the road; several uniformed men were standing about casually enough, but their attention was firmly fixed on her car. Since there was no real reason to drive further, she made a U-turn and went a half-mile back the way she'd come, just out of their sight. She pulled off the road and was presented with an unimpeded view of the Plain. She set the parking brake and got out for a look.

She was grateful for the lack of wind as she spread out the Ordnance Survey map on the bonnet and compared the land below with the contours on the map. There would have to be a slight modification of her proposed trail. The theoretical route of the stones would have used even less of the road than she'd originally estimated, and that shallow crease between two rounded hills would provide a gentle enough slope.

Satisfied that the map was accurate, she folded it so that the salient features could be seen at a glance, then slipped it into a pocket. She pulled the pair of cross-country skis she had rented out through the open passenger window, closed up and locked the car, leaving a note under the windscreen blade: "Broken down, will return with help presently."

It had been more years than she cared to remember since she'd been on skis. She had some difficulty recalling the knack of snapping them onto her boots, and no wonder! She laughed out loud. During her skiing days, dear Algie had always been right there to bend down and put them on for her. Handsome Algie, so athletic and always correct, perhaps too much so. He never would have approved of an unescorted lady off on her own like this. Her brief melancholy was immediately supplanted by a stubborn enjoyment of present independence. Algie had been long ago.

It took several gentle spills to get the hang of it again, but the actual decline of the terrain was so slight that it was easy to move along at a leisurely pace. It was really very much like walking, once one mastered the timing of the glissade between steps. She followed the natural downgrade, thanking heaven that her reserves of sprightliness were proving sufficient for the occasion. With a pause or two to catch her breath and consult the map and compass, she was soon in the sparse fringe of the wood that rolled down to the river. Here on the edge of the hard chalk, the trees were spaced far apart, and were stunted in comparison to those further down.

Lettie found a clearing well into the trees and decided to stop there for refreshment. She was well aware that a person her age should take frequent rests, although it was the only concession she made to old age.

With the practised eye of a veteran knitter, she was just estimating the distance between the closest trees, when a noise intruded on the peace of the clearing. Two nearby sparrows jerked their white-striped heads up in alarm, and quickly fluttered into the trees. Lettie remained where she was, in spite of an impulse to hide, since there wasn't anything she could do. She could not tell from where the scrape of skis cutting through snow was coming, but she had not been alone in the forest after all.

When he first appeared he seemed to be only a disembodied pink face. He was dressed all in white; even his automatic rifle, held casually at the ready, was colour-coordinated. He nodded to Lettie and did something to the weapon, creating another metallic clack, then swung it over his shoulder and looked past her. Another identically garbed man had emerged from the other side of the clearing.

"Good afternoon," she said, forcing a cheerful smile. These were two tough-looking customers, and she hadn't the faintest idea what to expect. The first man pushed back his white fur trimmed hood, revealing a jaunty blue beret decorated with a small bronze insignia. He shot a quick "bite on the bullet" look to his comrade, and that was the clue Lettie needed: it would have to be the scatty-old-thing routine. "Dear me, am I on government property?"

"No madam," Number One said, pulling out a small notebook and reading a series of numbers to her.

"Am I supposed to recognise those?" Her puzzled expression was genuine.

"It's the number plate on your red Volvo," Number One patiently explained.

"I'm afraid I've no head for numbers. I never have had, which is odd, since my cousin was a mathematician."

Number Two looked uncomfortable. It was easy to interpret the implicit message he was broadcasting to his companion—barracks room banter over this would be at their expense. He obviously wanted to get clear fast.

"We read your note and followed you down. You mentioned a breakdown."

"Oh yes. I hope that didn't make me look . . ."

"It did a bit," Number Two admitted impassively.

"I am so sorry! Well, are you lads out on an exercise? It certainly is a lovely day for it!"

There was a tense silence, then the leader seemed to make up his mind. "Yes, isn't it? If you'll just give us your name, I think we can be on our way. I don't see a breach of security here."

To their credit, both men managed to maintain official deadpan. It was not until they had disappeared like twin ghosts into the trees that she could hear the beginning of an angry exchange. It would have been interesting to follow and eavesdrop, but there were more urgent tasks requiring attention. She continued through the wood, closely examining the trunks of trees, at several spots taking out a tape measure and noting the distance between boles. As she made her observations she wondered if the soldiers would bother trying to verify the false name and address that she'd given them.

The river was quite broad at this point—just two miles downhill from the monument's site—and choked with a thick, slushy layer of ice that would soon melt enough to be swept away. Less than a mile further on she crossed a bridge that led directly to the footpath paralleling the old canal at the edge of Little Puddleton.

Crossing the bridge, she paused to admire this

fine example of the mason's art. It had a twin arch, the centre support being placed squarely in the middle of the river. This would normally have created a navigational blockade—each span was too narrow to allow the larger commercial barges to pass. But this problem was elegantly solved by the canal that diverted from the river at just this point. The lock—now in a sad state of neglect—that provided an entrance to the canal was part of the structure of the bridge itself. The old canal had originally proved a disappointment to its nineteenth-century builders, doing little to improve Little Puddleton's role as an industrial backwater, even though it just touched the edge of High Street at midpoint. Off-loading areas had been constructed, a dock, and a small artificial harbor. A second bridge had also been built at this point.

Unfortunately, no new wave of prosperity had materialised in that century. At first there was a brisk enough traffic of barges through the town, most transporting blocks of cut stone, but this trade soon trickled away. The quarries closed and the canal fell into disrepair.

From the first upstream bridge Lettie got a good view of the open lock, where the ice flowed through seamlessly, small puddles of water dotting its cloudy surface. The canal was probably shallower now than its original depth due to silt built up during a century of disuse. But as she neared the village, the pumps of the modern reclamation project could be heard filtering out the sand and mud from the harbour. From each of two temporary metal pump sheds a thick pipe could be seen leading over the side of the quay through the ice. The steady hammering was loud enough to drown out conversation in the immediate area, but once past the sheds the motors quickly faded into a gentle thrum. In the spring the park would be newly refurbished, and the pleasure craft (laden with hungry, knick-knack collecting tourists) would begin tying up at the dockside.

By teatime Lettie was wearily established in the tearoom, munching a stale biscuit and feeling very much her age. Already her muscles were stiffening from so much exertion. She would no doubt feel like Methuselah's great grannie by tomorrow, but the insights gained from the survey were undeniably worth every ache and pain. Hilsebeck banged the door, wrinkling his nose at the wee ersatz Highland decor. He slid into the booth across from her, saying, "Small wonder I never come in here. . . . Well, I hope my car didn't give you trouble."

"None, except that it's now on the military's list of suspicious vehicles."

"Not to worry, it's probably been there for days. They apprehended you?"

"Worse, I believe it's correct to say they 'got the drop on me.' Two youngsters on skis, toting rifles." A description of their uniforms caused the newsman's hazel eyes to rise from their habitual half mast.

"The blue cap goes with the Special Air Service. You know, the ones who staged that Iranian Embassy rescue in '81?"

"Yes, very competent boys. They didn't know what to do with *me*, though."

"That's not surprising." He laughed. An afternoon of sobering up at the office had brought back his good humour. "Any hope of hearing your wild theory now?"

"Yes, I'm now convinced it's plausible. Do you recall the discussion at lunch detailing how the ancients brought the stones all the way from Wales to Salisbury Plain?"

"It's a blur, but wasn't it mostly by sea and then in on the river?"

"You pass with high marks."

"I wasn't as besotted as I looked."

"I'm glad to hear it. Now, I remember reading somewhere that the easiest means of moving large weights is by water—even in these days of the Concorde."

"So you think the thieves took the stones down to the river then out to sea!" Even as he said it, he felt she had to be right. "You're a treasure," he declared, but there were terrible problems that made him dubious. "Isn't the river awfully shallow there?"

"Yes, but some barges only need a few inches of water."

"So that's all right. They must have come up river by motor barge under cover of the storm. But how the hell did they manage to get their equipment up the hill and the stones back down?"

"It seems difficult, I know," she sighed.

"Never mind. Maybe it'll come to you in a blinding flash while you're having your hair hennaed, or as you're looking for a nice piece of bream for dinner," he teased. It often happened that way in her novels.

"Let's hope so," was her solemn reply. "It would save a lot of fuss and bother."

"So once they accomplished the impossible and

got the stones down to the river bank, they must have loaded them into a barge and spirited them out to sea. They could be in Abu Dhabi by now." His tone said it was hopeless, but she seemed immune to despair.

"There's an interesting wrinkle here—the spans of the upstream bridge are too narrow for a barge to pass through. They would have had to use the canal past Little Puddleton."

"The bloody cheek! Floating right through the village. Still, in the middle of the blizzard, drifting with the current, the stones would have passed through quietly enough. . . . Don't I sound like a surgeon discussing some poor bloke's kidney?"

"Speaking of cheek," her eyes twinkling like the fairy godmother's just before she waved her magic wand, "I had a lovely gossip with a local dog owner this afternoon. Such a friendly gentleman, he's in the habit of running his spaniel along the full length of the canal and down part of the river every morning. I asked him when it had frozen completely. He said that the day before the storm there was only a thin layer of ice. Then he and his poor pet were housebound for three days due to the blizzard. On the fourth day when they ventured out again the ice was quite uniformly thick all the way across both canal and river."

"And what bearing does this have on the case? The stones are long gone."

"Perhaps not. The seas would have been very rough. The weather was so beastly I don't imagine they could have managed it during the actual storm. . . . And if they'd taken them since, the ice would have been noticeably disturbed. My spaniel man says it hasn't been."

J.D. leaned forwards, sputtering in his agitation. "Then . . . well I'll be damned."

"Yes, they're probably still lying on the bottom of the canal. The ice is thawing . . . I expect the pirates will retrieve their treasure some night soon."

"Where in the canal? And why the canal rather than the river? Unless a muddy bottom would have created problems."

She shrugged. "Your guess is as good as mine. It's impossible to see anything through the ice just yet; but I'd certainly place my bet on the canal." Lettie sounded convinced.

He absentmindedly fumbled through his pockets for a cigarette, too excited to remember that he was all out. "Let me think this through. If you're right . . . we ought to call that Yank newspaper and tell them to start drafting us a cheque . . . then we should notify the police to cordon off the area. On the other hand, if you're wrong the press will make us look like a pair of bungling idiots. Today I am still Australia's gift to mankind, but let me make one slip and the papers will revel in showing me up for an ass. If it's one thing the press loves better than creating heroes, it's exposing their feet of clay."

"Dear, dear! Yes, I'm afraid that you've got . . . ." She faded off, uncomfortably sharing her partner's anticipation of public humiliation. It wouldn't do her image as a mystery writer any good. But more bitter still was picturing Gwenna Hardcastle eating bonbons and chuckling over Lettie's fall. Not that Lettie had any evidence that Dame Gwenna was the sort of mean-spirited old baggage who would laugh at such a thing, but it seemed very likely. Nemeses were like that.

"There's only one thing to do," J.D. suddenly declared, breaking through her unhappy reverie. "I'm going home and hit the sack."

"What? You're going to pull the blankets over your head like some—" She could think of no epithet disapproving enough. What was youth coming to?

"Wait, now! I must have a nap if I'm going to stay awake. Tonight I'll be out on the canal. I'll take along some sort of pole and see if I can sound the bottom. It might be possible to locate the stones that way."

"That's the spirit! But do be very careful!" she pleaded. It was one thing for her to ski through a cordon of rifle-packing military police. That was in broad daylight, and she had her whimsical protective colouring to get her through. What did this mere boy across the table have to protect him should he come up against unscrupulous burglars in the dead of night? "My dear John David, have you a revolver?"

He laughed, making light of her concern, then changing the subject. "By the way, I've been doing some follow up on Nordstromson, just seeing what talk was going around. It was mostly the usual rumours about his amorous appetites. . . ." He waited to see what effect the remark would have. But Lettie didn't bat an eyelash, so he continued. "The other day someone saw Nordstromson talking to a foreign-looking charlie in a black Mercedes with diplomatic plates."

"Well?"

"That's all. It's just that diplomatic plates are an oddity around here. What would Nordstromson be doing talking to—"

"It could be a visiting friend," she interrupted, obviously unimpressed. "Or a stranger asking directions. Tourists do that, you know."

"Tourists don't swan about in foreign embassy cars."

"Foreign embassy employees out seeing the sights might. I'm sorry, but I don't find anything particularly sigificant in this. Could it be that you resent Nordstromson and are just looking for something to pin on him because of it?"

"It could be," J.D. said without shame. "But Devereux's got nothing personal against him, and I hear he's been asking a lot of questions about the Swede's activities."

"Who is Devereux?"

"A London reporter, and our rival in the hunt. He bears watching, believe me!"

It was extremely peaceful in Little Puddleton, but then, it wasn't the sort of place that would be lively on a winter's night—especially well after midnight. A dense fog blanketed the landscape, thickest above the canal and harbour. From Hilsebeck's perch on the bridge over the canal, the glow from the nearby street lamps was just sufficient to enable him to see a few feet in all directions. It was darkest under the bridge and in the unlit park.

There was no doubt about it, the mercury was rising, as the warm temperatures of the nearby seacoast slowly moved back the cold inland air. A few cracks and groans from the slushy ice indicated that the harder stuff underneath was breaking up.

He did some poking around with a billiard cue, the closest thing he could find to a barge pole at this time of year. He wanted to sound the bottom of the canal, hoping to find discrepancies in depth that might indicate mammoth stones lying in the mud. But the cue wasn't long enough; he soon gave it up and curled into his sleeping bag against the side of the bridge. If Lettie's theory was correct, he would be standing all-night vigils until something broke.

The steady hum of the pumps provided a background to the creaking of the ice sheets. The eerie rolling fog moved out towards the north, leaving the air damp and still.

He waited, shuffling through the random thoughts of someone alone and trying to stay awake.

After a while the same old mental menu began to lose its appeal. All he wanted to do was sleep. It would be so easy just to close his eyes and drift off. He jerked awake again, his whole body starting slightly. He was a voracious sleeper; he had long hinted to all and sundry that his frequent naps were lingering symptoms of a blackwater dengue picked up in Malaya. The first person he'd approached with this excuse had been his mother, who wasn't impressed. She knew that her eight-year-old hadn't even been to Melbourne, let alone the Malay Peninsula.

Yawning, he did a few sit-ups, then crawled out of his bag. He stretched to his toes, careful not to step out of the shadows. He wanted a cigarette, but was reluctant to risk the telltale glow. Time crawled by. He was about to throw caution to the wind and have a smoke when his eye suddenly caught a light moving towards him.

It looked like a narrow-beamed flashlight, darting about in the fog with the almost frantic motions he associated with a freshly released dog just out of the house and looking for trouble. Hilsebeck crouched down behind the wrought iron grating of the bridge and peered into the gloom. The light was rapidly approaching, but it was impossible to make out the carrier. Heart hammering, J.D. crouched, as he heard running footsteps beneath the bridge immediately below him.

From that moment events moved swiftly in the murk that obscured practically everything but sound. There came a sad moan, unearthly, too loud and drawn out to come from any human throat— the voice of a giant having a nightmare. Icy spiders scurried down Hilsebeck's neck as he leaned over the bridge, trying to tell what was going on. There was a large black shape rising up out of the canal. The length of several motor cars, it seemed to be growing with every new groan and splash. The flashlight flicked back on, revealing a rectangular block of ice rising upwards, surrounded by what appeared to be the rounded black hump of a sea serpent. The effect was so peculiar that for a moment J.D. could make no sense of it.

A tall figure bundled up in a dark coat and hat stepped out from under the bridge. He ran his light across another block that was rising with the crack and squeal of splitting ice sheets. A light bulb went on in Hilsebeck's brain—surely this was Stonehenge coming up from the ooze! So Lettie had been right. But there was no time to marvel; he'd better nip off and call the cops.

He stealthily crept across the bridge, filled with an increasing sense of urgency. He was making his way towards the village when a horrible, high-pitched scream stopped him in his tracks. The scream was followed by an awful crunching noise. For a moment he just stood still, uncertain what to do. Should he investigate the scream? But what could he do alone, unarmed, stumbling around in the dark? No, there was nothing for it but to call the police.

As he was running past the pumphouse, the sea-serpent shape suddenly made sense—it had to be some kind of flotation device, probably inflated from a machine in this shed. The door was slightly ajar, a pale stream of light outlining the inside. J.D. hesitated once more, telling himself it would be foolhardy to risk a look. He moved on, and was congratulating himself for a cool head triumphing over the superstitious terror that was gripping his insides, when a deep, dark hole opened at his feet. He fell, trying to cry out—but a heavy weight pushed all the air out of his lungs.

J.D. awoke to the pale light of dawn, as well as to a rhythmic hammering through his body that at first seemed to be coming from the pump next to his ear. But this device was quite silent. The painful pounding was the pulsing of blood through his head. He groaned aloud, miserably aware of a million discomforts. First priority was to roll over to avoid the piercing light from the little window. He was wet, cold, and from the acid smell that cut through the pong of grease and ozone from the motors, he could tell he'd been sick all over himself.

The difficulty of achieving a sitting position made apparent the main source of his acute misery—he was trussed up hand and foot like a Christmas goose. Or a prize dodo—even in his present state of muzzy-headedness, humiliation was all too vivid. The open door had been such an obvious lure. The contents of his wallet lay around him on the wet concrete floor.

Kicking against the door and shouting relieved a little frustration and eventually attracted the early rising spaniel and his owner. Not that Hilsebeck's calls could be heard as far as the village. The nice gentleman had only come closer to find out why "them blasted machines 'ad stopped." Only in silence had the two little sheds drawn attention.

Hilsebeck limped out, slightly behind the spaniel man, who was staring into the canal and remarking, "Well, ain't that somethin'? All the ice is gone over night. What do you suppose could have done that?"

J.D. considered ramming his head against the side of the building, but decided not to—one concussion was enough. He settled for emitting a string of curses in his native Australian that left his rescuer alarmed, convinced he'd let loose a madman. This old gentleman apparently didn't recognise what was perfectly normal behaviour for someone just comprehending that Stonehenge had slipped through his fingers.

7

"YOU KNOW HOW PRACTICAL JOKERS ARE—especially under the influence of a quart of gin," was Hilsebeck's frothy response to his rescuer, who inquired how he'd gotten himself tied up in the pump shed. "I never should have ribbed old Jack about his team losing the football match. But he meant no harm; we've been cobbers since school." He began to edge away from those scrutinising eyes. The man's pooch was playfully yanking at the loosened ropes that had fallen at Hilsebeck's feet.

"That's one nasty bump on your temple," the other man remarked, obviously not fooled by J.D.'s shaky show of unconcern.

"It's nothing. Well, I'd better toddle or I'll be late for work. Thanks again for coming to my aid. . . . That's a tiptop spaniel you've got there—I bet he's a stunning hunter. . . ." He waved and made good his escape. As quickly as his thundering head would allow, he walked to the Blue Man and rented a room. It was a matter of lying down immediately, or falling down. He didn't even consider attempting the six-mile drive to his own flat in Amesbury.

After a bout of nausea, J.D. lay flat on his back and dialled the nearest police. Chief Constable

Coggs himself answered on the fifteenth ring. It was a few minutes before seven, and it sounded like the old bull had just walked in the door without benefit of his first cup of tea. "Hilsebeck? What the bloody hell do you want now?"

"To do you a good turn, Chief. I suggest you bring a couple men down here to Little Puddleton and comb the vicinity in and around the canal. If you stumble across anything interesting, you'll find me in room sixteen at the Blue Man. We might be able to strike a bargain."

"Don't play games with me, you young monkey! I've got better things to do than waste the morning on some wild goose chase."

"I don't expect you'll find a goose; more likely a dead duck." He hung up and covered his eyes with a pillow. Why had he said that? Not just to tantalize the old bear into action, although it would surely accomplish that. He hadn't even thought of it until he'd heard himself say it, but once spoken the realisation was unavoidable. Someone had probably died.

"Good hunting?" J.D. asked offhandedly. It was only half past nine. The chief wouldn't have been sitting here by his bed so soon unless he'd discovered something.

"That's a pretty bit of work on your crumpet." Coggs smirked. "No doubt earned by mooching around with your finger up your nose."

J.D. said that he refused to make any comment until informed what the police had found. A volley of veiled—and unveiled—threats from both sides eventually brought Coggs around to admitting that they had discovered a body. "Male, crushed beyond all recognition. We found him tangled in the hose line, floating in the canal."

"Crushed! The poor devil! Caught between a rock and a hard place." J.D. shuddered, then recalling the height of the man in the fog, asked, "Not blond, was he?" When Coggs ignored that question he fired another one at him. "How long will it take to identify the body?" But the chief only shrugged and demanded to know what J.D. had to say. "Not much," J.D. replied. "I have no idea who the poor blighter was. I'm not sure if it was an accident or not. But I'll bet you dollars to doughnuts that his death had something to do with Stonehenge."

"Stonehenge!" Coggs' furry eyebrows disappeared under his sparse thatch of red hair. His piggy eyes grew round, then narrowed. "You did say Stonehenge?"

"Yeah, the purloined rocks themselves. Hidden under the ice. They were brought up from the bottom last night, crushing that poor bugger in the process. At least I presume all the stones were there—I only got a look at one."

Coggs made outraged noises, but finally gained control long enough to demand, "I want to know how the bloody hell you—"

"I was there when it happened, although I didn't actually see the man die. I couldn't see much of anything—but I heard the scream. I was going for help when someone coshed me. When I woke up I was tied to a pump and the fait was accompli."

"What were you doing out there at that time of night?"

"Trying to prove a wild theory that otherwise would have sounded like just another crazy idea. I could hardly believe it myself when I saw that thing

76

pop up out of the ice! I thought I was hallucinating!"

The cop digested this for several minutes, all the while turning a deeper shade of scarlet. J.D. pulled the pillow around his ears to muffle the fierce rain of invectives that followed. Finally Coggs ran down enough for J.D. to drag a few more tit-bits out of him. Most significantly, he learned that a team of naval divers would be arriving that afternoon to search the canal.

After the chief had gone, J.D. picked up the phone and dialled the newspaper. To his editor he dictated the bare bones of last night's events, suggesting that the headline banner should be: MUTILATED BODY—WAS IT STONEHENGE? Jenks was beside himself with joy. "Oh, buck up son! It's better that you couldn't stop them. This will drag out the story for weeks. If you'd been the big hero and caught the buggers red-handed this early in the game, we'd have nothing but the weather report to put on the front page next week."

Hilsebeck uttered something obscene and hung up. He lay in bed another hour, nursing his head and brooding over the poisonous ink Devereux and the rest of his esteemed colleagues would surely make of the story. Of course he would scoop them with his eyewitness account. But tomorrow they would get their revenge by emphasising his impotence in the whole affair. So what if he had been on the spot—he'd bungled it, hadn't he?

More bitter than the thought of Devereux's gloating over his failure was the awful realisation that Lettie and he had just lost their edge in the treasure hunt. As soon as the edition was out this afternoon, a mob of fortune hunters would be on the scent of Stonehenge, last seen heading down the Avon. He would have to come up with a generous dose of daily codswallop to muddy the waters. It would be a simple matter to make good use of the bogus claims that would be pouring in: STONES SPOTTED AT BRIGHTON PIER. Or: "Mrs. Cribbage of Eelling informed authorities today that her neighbour stole Stonehenge and buried it in his garden."

But was there any hope of keeping everybody going round in circles by reporting several sightings a day at far-flung points of the globe? Not bloody likely. Feeling extremely miserable, he dialled Lettie's room. She was only a few doors away, but he hadn't contacted her. No use putting it off any longer—he would have to break the news of his failure.

Lettie was there in seconds, her sympathy placing heavy emphasis on woolly afghans and tea laced with brandy. "You mustn't go on cursing yourself," she scolded, tucking the afghan up to his chin. "It will do no good and probably bring on pneumonia. We'll still manage to find the stones—they've only eluded us for the moment."

J.D. groaned, unable to think of an optimistic response. He looked out the window at the grey tendrils of fog weaving past the tall cedars that stood between the inn and the back of the church. "If it was murder—if someone pushed him—it raises a bothersome question."

"Yes, why are you still . . ."

"Alive. It does give one pause." He pursed his lips and abstractedly made little putt-putt noises. She offered him more tea, but he wanted straight brandy instead. He took a sip and closed his eyes wearily. "One more interesting detail. My wallet wasn't where it should have been. Somebody took it out—no doubt to check my ID."

"They know who you are, then."

"And, more's the pity, *we* don't know who *they* are. Except our Swede, possibly. Any sign of him?" he asked. Lettie said that she would find out.

She soon rose, saying she must do some gossiping with the locals. "Why don't you try to get some rest? It will do you a world of good." What a sorry sight he was! Those blue circles under his eyes and that nasty brownish yellow lump! "And I will have a physician come look at you straight away. You don't look at all well." She patted his hand and they arranged to meet later in the day if he was up to it.

At one on the dot Hilsebeck was unsteadily descending the narrow flight of stairs to the lobby of the inn, a commodious hodge-podge of dark beams and well-polished brass what-nots, all dimly lit by the few shafts of weak sunlight that angled through mullioned panes. His vision had that preternatural sharpness he associated with the day after a binge. Dancing motes of dust flashed like orbiting suns in a shaft of light. The threads on the bare spots in the old carpet were as well-defined as the warp and woof of his own tweed jacket. All in all, it was good to be among the living.

He sipped black coffee and stared vaguely at the tintype advertisements hanging on the wall, trying to muster the will to continue the investigation. His morose contemplations were curtailed by the appearance of Lettie's frail form on the arm of Julia's superb one. He watched as they crossed the room towards him. The bump on his head had knocked the habitual mist from his eyes. He felt as if he were watching a film, and this was a scene imbued with significance: The Day After the Tragedy, Take 1, Quiet Please. Lettie, in a navy cape over a matching skirt and boots, was moving stiffly. It made her look very fragile. He wondered how old she was. Julia was wearing a fuzzy white turtleneck pullover and russet-coloured trousers. She was moving with a sinuous stride, in spite of having to go slowly for her aunt's benefit. He was very glad to see her.

"What did the surgeon say about your head?" Julia cheerily inquired.

"Just major brain damage." He shrugged.

"Nothing serious then," she quipped.

"That's good news," Lettie exclaimed. "We were worried about you, dear boy. I'm glad to see the pink back in your cheeks."

"I think I'll survive, thank you."

"This is turning into a beastly business," Lettie murmured.

"Yes, especially for the dead man," was J.D.'s response.

"Was it murder?" Lettie asked.

"I can't say," he replied. "He might have been pushed in. There wasn't much clearance between the canal and the stones. And one stone had gone mad, tottering and jumping up out of the water like Nessie in front of a sleeping photographer." He took a moment to try to sort it out with what was left of his mind. "On the other hand, it could have been just a horrible accident. Conditions were poor for the job."

"But if it was murder, I should think they'd be anxious to remove the body," Julia said.

"It was tangled in the air lines they used to inflate

their flotation devices. They used the canal clean-up project as a disguise for their own hoses. Clever boys," he added.

"But who is the dead man?"

There was a lengthy silence. None of them had enough experience with death to be able to discuss it lightly.

"Anybody local missing?" J.D. directed at Lettie.

Lettie shook her head. "But it's too early yet for anybody to be considered missing."

"Seen Nordstromson around anywhere?" He kept it casual.

"Surely you don't think . . ." Julia gasped.

"Not to worry, he's probably in the sack some-where with one of his dollies," he heard himself saying. I really am wowing her with my sophistica-tion, he thought miserably. At that point she made an ambiguous announcement that she intended to make certain that Nordstromson really was in bed with somebody and walked out. "Ouch," he said, rubbing his tender head.

Lettie gave him a reproachful look, but refrained from giving any advice about Julia. It was too bad he persisted in handling it all wrong, but it was none of her business. "It has just occurred to me that the victim might be one of the thieves," she said, sticking to the business at hand.

"If so, he's probably from out of town."

She agreed. "But, if he wasn't one of the thieves, he might still be an outsider. And if he didn't come up the river on a boat, how else would he get here? In this small a place, I should think a taxi would be. . ."

"We could check that out easily enough."

"Or the victim might have driven his own car,

which would still be sitting around somewhere. Wouldn't you think that an unfamiliar vehicle left overnight might be noticed?" He said that it was a possibility they ought to pursue. "Let's," she said. "It'll cheer us both up to be out and about."

J.D. said he could do with some cheering.

It wasn't a car, but a shabby van parked illegally in front of a certain Mrs. McNeary's cottage. This formidable creature answered the bell on the first ring, as if lurking just inside, like a fat spider ready to pounce on its prey. "Well, if this is your wreck," she tossed a contemptuous glance in the direction of the offending vehicle, "you're just too late!" The object in question was a tatty old Morris Minor van, sprayed flat black.

"Get the number—and anything else fast!" he mumbled in Lettie's ear, then confronted this nasty bit of work with his best boyish smile. "Such a nuisance, taking up all the space in front of your cottage! Who could blame you for—"

"Don't come that nicey-nice tone with me," she snapped like one who'd grown plump on a steady diet of salesmen. "I've called the coppers, and they're going to be here any minute to tow that hulk of yours out to sea!"

"We'll gladly drive it away," J.D. insinuated smoothly, confident he could hot-wire it in seconds. A little car theft would round out the afternoon nicely. He edged closer and tried the door. Locked! Blast! Meanwhile Lettie was quietly wandering around the back.

"Won't do no good. I let the air out of yer tires."

He let a howl of protest escape his lips as he looked down at her flaccid victims. "Why you bloody old cow!" That got her full attention. Her jaw dropped. "And with Uncle Albert in there!"

"You cheeky bastard!" she yelled, with a mixture of indignation and relish. "Don't you call me a bloody cow! So who's Uncle Albert?"

"Apparently you didn't break in and have a look. Too bad the doors were locked, or you'd have got a jolly surprise."

"Are you threatening me?" she demanded, squaring her shoulders, her chins quivering dangerously. "You'd better tell me about this Uncle Albert."

"*Her* Albert, in here." He pointed at Lettie with one hand while pounding on the roof of the van with the other. "Dead."

"No!" Unabashed native curiosity drew her a step farther off her porch. "Does *she* know?" she whispered, eyeing Lettie who was gazing through the passenger's window, oblivious to the conversation.

"Not a thing, anymore. Right off her head with grief. Just look at her." Mrs. McNeary needed no encouragement. She was hooked now, sucked in by a juicy story that showed great promise. Unfortunately, the cops chose that moment to intervene. J.D. spotted them immediately—a police cruiser nosing into the street, the driver consulting a map. He was one of Coggs' boys, direct from Amesbury. "Aunt Ivy, don't!" J.D. cried dramatically, hustling around to the other side of the van and grabbing hold of Lettie's shoulder. Lettie looked appropriately startled. "I must get her back to the sanitorium right away. She isn't strong," he added, emotion choking his voice. "Cops!" he hissed at his sidekick. "Let's scarper." They did.

They reached the waterside in time to see the divers entering the canal. The entire area was mobbed with onlookers. Just an hour ago there had been no sign of the media. But now that the *Plain Speaker* had been out for an hour, the press had descended in force, hoping that something worth a few inches of front page might be gleaned from the dive. Hilsebeck spotted Devereux hanging on the side-lines, intent on buttonholing one of the divers whose head was just sticking out of the water.

Lettie and J.D. found a relatively uncrowded spot on the bridge, if one ingored the Japanese camera buffs who were using the railing as a support for their video camera. They were festooned with light meters, videocassette machines, and tape recorders bulging from their pockets.

Below, the police effectively kept anyone from walking under the bridge. A small work crew of pa-trolmen, stripped to their singlets, were wrestling with the Laocoön coils of dark air pipe that was being pulled out of the water. A diver surfaced with a splash, put something on the edge of the bank, then swam across to his pal, tapping him on a rubbery shoulder, and pointing down with an em-phatic gesture. Lettie and her partner exchanged significant looks. The two divers disappeared back into the water in a swirl of bubbles. Their twin search beams were only discernible for a moment; visibility must be pretty poor down there.

"Notice the police," Lettie intoned.

"Oh, yes—the old sleight of hand."

The police threw a blanket over the find, then put it into an opaque plastic evidence bag. There were a pile of bags already, all lumped together at Constable Coggs' feet. This in itself wasn't par-ticularly significant: they would collect every old boot and tin can, then sort it out later. Trouble was this evidence would be off-limits to reporters; so everyone present was elbowing to get a look before it was covered up.

Hilsebeck turned around in response to a nudge in the ribs. One of the Orientals had inadvertently backed into him while taking a picture of his comrades. J.D. took a closer look at the man's camera— one of the newest gee-whiz toys from Transistor Land, an all-in-one unit, much like the ancient movie camera his father had used. But this one had replaced the old-fashioned film with a videocassette. He could see the little sprockets turning on the side as the tape advanced. The Japanese murmured something that sounded apologetic in his native tongue and smiled shyly, pointing to the camera. J.D. bowed, all hands-across-the-sea. He had an idea.

His pantomimed interest elicited the expected offer to look through the viewfinder. Hilsebeck accepted the device with much smiling and nodding, all the while noting that the controls were in universal symbols as well as Japanese pictographs.

J.D. put it to his eye and focused on the scene below, initially surprised to notice a miniature television screen an inch or two from his right eye. "My, my . . . what will they think of next?" he purred, finding the zoom lever and watching the scene enlarge. A diver's head emerged, shedding droplets like a seal; the image filled the screen. Discreetly releasing the pause button, he kept the diver's hand centered on the screen as the motor began to turn. The excited swimmer waved a sodden handful, then gently placed his find on the ground. J.D. tried to follow his actions from above, panning too far to the right and getting a nice full screen shot of a policeman's boot. He corrected back, and saw the unidentifiable object for only a fraction of a second before a blanket fell over it. He watched for another moment, but nothing else was revealed. Pretending to be just playing, he brought the camera around, taking a picture of Lettie.

There was a tap on his shoulder; the nice man wanted his camera back. Hilsebeck hit the eject button. With the clack of well-oiled hinges a little door opened; the cassette clattered next to his feet. Feigning dismay he quickly stooped as if to pick it up, neatly blocking the way for the Japanese, who lunged forward after his tape. The reporter groped in his pocket, grabbing the first thing that came to hand and dropped it next to the cassette, which was now covered by the flaps of his overcoat. He neatly palmed the tape, then kicked the object from his pocket over the side. It made a convincing splash below.

The next few moments strained international relations. They were all still smiling, but somehow it didn't seem quite the same. His face drawn into an exaggerated grimace of apology, Hilsebeck handed the camera back, then pointed to the men in the water. The Japanese caught on fast, waving and shouting at the divers. One navy man got the message in spite of the language barrier and obligingly swam over and dove in the spot they indicated. Hilsebeck faded from the scene, Lettie right behind him, lest the frustrated Orientals forget their manners and toss him over the side after their lost film.

"Well done, John David," Lettie said, chuckling, as they made good their escape. "Now how are we going to view your home movie?"

"I believe there's a place in Amesbury that rents camera equipment. . . Oh hell!" he cried, going through his pockets. "I'll have to hot-wire my car. It was my keys that I kicked over the bridge!"

"This should do nicely," Hilsebeck remarked, pushing open the chromium-trimmed glass door of Tech Video. Indirect lighting, polished aluminum, and wine-coloured carpet produced a plush ambience. The equipment was displayed in dark recesses, their ruby red lights glowing. To Lettie, who had never had anything more space-aged than her recently acquired microwave, the whole display had a science-fiction quality of lost jewelled cities buried in velvet-lined subterranean caverns. The effect was very striking, if slightly disorienting.

A willowy salesman emerged from the back and raised a dubious eyebrow. He emanated arrogance and a faint trace of boredom that seemed to complement his sleek Monte Carlo suit and supercilious face. "Good evening?"

"I understand that you have rentals," J.D. said.

"Rentals?" A slight up and down glance at Hilsebeck, then Lettie, then back to Hilsebeck. "Very well," he sighed, turning on his heel. "This way, please." He floated behind a counter and touched a button that illuminated a large collection of videocassettes. "All rentals are a minimum of twenty-four hours. There is a deposit of five pounds, refundable upon return." He grabbed a handful of boxes and dropped them onto the countertop. Lettie picked one up and read aloud. "Le Sex Shop." She looked bemused.

"What kind of place *is* this?" J.D. demanded.

"A specialty shop. Perhaps this isn't quite what

you and your . . . companion here had in mind?" The salesman's tone was ironic.

"No, as a matter of fact, we wanted to rent some playback equipment," J.D. replied, gesturing at the displays of posh gadgets. "Do you rent this stuff, or is it just cover for your porn business?"

"I'm sorry, sir, we don't rent equipment. We sell it."

"Very well, I'd like to see a demonstration of the model that plays this kind of cassette."

"Ah, the VHS system—very nice indeed. It records in three different speed ranges, you know."

"That's wonderful, why don't you show us how it works." The salesman bowed and led them to a large unit with incandescent green numerals. He inserted the tape and the machine whirred to life.

"And how does one run it back a bit?" J.D. wanted to know.

"Very simple; notice that we can monitor the progress as we rewind." He indicated a colour television set in a niche above the recorder where figures jerked rapidly backwards, like a reversed Keystone Kops chase.

"Stop it right there." The picture reverted to a normal forward pace, showing the smiling, posturing Japanese. "Little party we had," said the reporter.

"Very nice grain," the clerk remarked, closely scrutinising the screen. "Bit of miscalibration; that would be the tape skew." He made a minor adjustment with a control knob. "Ah, much better."

The scene with the diver came on now, zooming in; the focus was good. "Is there some way we could stop it right there?" asked Lettie.

"Easiest thing in the world." The salesman

handed her a remote control unit. "Just press the pause button. You can also move forwards or back frame by frame." He indicated the appropriate buttons.

She made appreciative sounds as the diver's hand came out of the water and deposited the soggy object on the bank. She froze the frame, her chin jutting eagerly forwards. "How very, very. . ."

"It looks like somebody lost his toupeé while taking a dip," the clerk whinnied.

"Yes, some party that was," Hilsebeck said, not quite knowing what to make of Lettie's obvious elation. "Well, this is a charming piece of equipment that I can't possibly live without. I'll be back on payday."

The salesman shrugged indifferently, recognising a lie when he heard one. This brazen twit had been a disappointment all around. But the old lady seemed mad keen on it, and looked the sort to have a nice bundle in her sock drawer. A bit crackers though, he decided as they departed with their tape, the old girl going on and on about false beards. Of all things.

8

THE TWO DETECTIVES parted ways. Hilsebeck returned to his office in Amesbury and put in several hours making telephone inquiries about Nordstromson.

The *Plain Speaker*'s dead-article file produced a tantalising paragraph on a group of archaeologists that had petitioned the National Trust a year before. They had wanted to excavate under Stonehenge, which would have made it necessary to temporarily move the stones. The petition had been rejected. In a recent lecture to the local historical society, Nordstromson had described that decision as "a fine example of dunderhead logic."

J.D. mulled over this potentially scientific motivation for the heist as he strolled over to the police station to see Chief Constable Coggs, who was showing increasing signs of strain. In the past several days the chief's office had been filling up with paperwork resulting from the British public's need to accuse and confess. Mail and phone calls from all over England had to be recorded and responded to. Some four hundred odd souls were claiming to have the stones held for ransom, the fee ranging from a mere two hundred pounds to sums that would tax the national treasury into oblivion. These demands, being potential fraud, required greater attention from the Yard. But as the officer concerned, Coggs received all of these official reports in triplicate. Wading through them was out of the question, considering his own manpower problems, yet he was responsible for responding to each. When J.D. entered the office, Coggs was floundering in a frustrated effort to find room to store all the reports.

"Can you guess how many man hours this represents? Can you imagine what is involved in checking four hundred official reports just on ransom demands?" the chief moaned, waving a fistful of paper.

"No I can't," J.D. said.

"Neither can I. All I know is that it's going to take more time and more men than I have."

The reporter shook his head empathetically, feeling slightly ill as he considered the ransom motivation for the first time. It was a most viable motive—and beyond the limits of a one man–one woman amateur detective team. If the monument had indeed been stolen for monetary gain, only the authorities would have access to communications from the thieves, and only they could investigate from that angle. He was momentarily so discouraged that he was tempted just to go away quietly without bothering to blackmail information out of the chief. Only the thought of his partner's persistent, cheery pluck shamed him into carrying on.

"Have you heard the rumoured identity of the Swede's snow-bunny on that fateful day?" J.D. half-heartedly insinuated. The colour of Coggs' face said that he had. His own daughter! If that little titbit was published the chief constable would never live it down.

"What do you want, you slimy snake in the grass?"

"Was the corpse blond?"

"That's become your favourite question. Regrettably, no."

"So our Swede is still with us. I don't suppose there's any standing charge against him? A traffic offense? Paternity suit? Ah well."

"Why are you after Nordstromson?" Coggs asked.

"Nothing concrete yet, just a gut feeling." J.D. sighed.

"I don't have time for wishful thinking. What were you doing sniffing around that abandoned van in Little Puddleton?"

"I had a hunch it might have belonged to the dead man. What do you say?"

There was a silence while Coggs considered the pros and cons of tossing him a bone. The pros won this time, since the bone was puny. "The plates were off an old wreck. We might be able to trace them. Our lab boys are crawling all over the vehicle with tweezers and microscopes."

"I'd love to know what they find."

"I bet you would," came the ironic reply.

"I'll trade you my info on Nordstromson for your report on the van."

"What info?"

Sorry, but you've caught me in the middle of making further inquiries."

The policeman snorted. "I know what *that* means!"

"Well then, I'll be certain to give you a tinkle the

moment I get anything. And I bet you know what *that* means too!" He left, gratified with having the last word this round.

Back at the office J.D. looked over his notes from an interview he'd done on the Swede shortly after the theft. At the time he had intended on writing a short profile of the man who'd discovered Stonehenge missing. Now that he was looking at him in a more suspicious light, he decided to check up on the archaeologist's credentials. It was the sort of credibility check that should have taken less than an hour of chatting up personnel clerks on the phone. But this time nobody would confirm or deny any sort of connection to Gunnar Nordstromson. J.D. was forced to give up when both the Royal Geographic Society and the Fellows of the British Museum brushed him off with, "I'm sorry, but we are not authorized to give out that information."

The reporter gulped down a couple of aspirins and lay back in his chair to do some serious ruminating. Just before he fell asleep, he concluded that either the Swede was a phony or the world's only top-secret archaeologist.

The phone brought him out of his slumber. It was the night editor wanting to know where his Stonehenge story was for tomorrow. J.D. threw together a gothic rehash that Jenks would surely throw in his face, come the morning. It couldn't be helped. He had no intention of giving helpful hints to fellow rock hounds.

He dropped the story on the night editor's desk and bundled up to face the night. There was just time to drive over to Nordstromson's cottage before heading for home. He left his car a block away and crunched over the snowy sidewalk, gingerly skirting pools of ice. The cul-de-sac that went past Twee's Company, the dingy little brick horror that the Swede rented, was deserted. Everybody was inside their homes at this hour, tucking into their evening sausages and watching Dave Allen at large on their small screens.

There was a sliver of light outlining Nordstromson's drawn shade. Had the rooster returned to roost at last? Whistling loudly, J.D. mounted the rickety wooden steps. A scrambling sound came from within, followed by a door banging around the back. J.D. vaulted over the rail and ran, slipping on a frozen patch in the garden. By the time he reached the rear, he just caught a glimpse of someone disappearing behind the houses at the end of the lane. A dog woofed from inside one of them. J.D. skidded to a halt, unwilling to risk more concussions. There was nothing but dark gardens behind those dwellings, then the woods beyond.

The flapping kitchen door provided a more attractive prospect. He slipped through the ship-shape kitchenette into the main room, which showed signs of ransacking. Books lay in a jumble on the floor. Drawers were pulled out. A reading lamp illuminated a pile of relief maps and charts.

As he was poking through the debris a loud click made him start, but it was only the sound of a cassette player coming to a halt, the rewind button still pressed down. So this was what the intruder had been doing when interrupted. J.D. listened to part of the tape, but learned nothing except that it was in a foreign language.

An unusual map on the wall caught his attention—a special aerial map of the entire Salisbury Plain, including the military preserve. The details were remarkably clear, right down to the lattices of the antennae on the radar vans drawn in a circle. He could even read the SAAB radiator emblems on the trucks. On the back of the document "Most Secret" was stamped in red. Hardly the sort of thing an archaeologist ought to have hanging next to his desk!

The telephone book of the Salisbury Military District was another anomaly. What was this classified material doing beside a civilian's phone? J.D. thumbed through it, stopping at a page listing Operational Headquarters. On impulse, he dialled the only number that was underlined: O.R.B. extension 647. A voice answered, "Red Blinder."

"So sorry," J.D. mumbled and rang off. He was pawing through the stuff on the desk when he heard a vehicle stop out front and the sound of boots pounding up to the front door in military unison. J.D. stuffed papers in his pocket with one hand and fumbled at the cassette machine with the other. No time! With a last desperate grab he settled for bagging the cassette's storage box and bolted out the kitchen door.

The women arrived at Hilsebeck's flat only minutes after he had. "Do come in. Sorry it's such a pigsty," his arm swept across the cluttered room, "but boys will be boys."

"Quite all right," Lettie assured him, looking around uncertainly for a place to sit.

"Sorry!" their host said, scooping up an armful of brochures to clear the couch. "Thanks for answering my summons."

Julia helped, glancing at the pictures as she piled them onto the overloaded coffee table. "Yachts, airplanes? Planning on coming into a lot of cash soon?"

"Counting on it. But I'm feeling the terrible responsibility. I lie awake nights trying to decide what sort of plane to get. Or would a yacht be more practical? Then there's the time-consuming business of acquiring the requisite number of polo ponies."

Lettie was the one to bring them down to business. "I've inquired at the Blue Man. The dead man definitely wasn't a former guest there. I also checked the cab companies and found no record of a fare to the village in anything like the right time frame. And neither of us has yet located Nordstromson."

"Odd how elusive our Swede is. I came up with only one definite fact on him today. He isn't the one who died in the canal. I found out little else about him, though, except that he had at least two unwelcome visitors at his cottage tonight, yours truly being the second."

"Who was the first?" they chorused.

"I can't be certain. I got only a quick look, but I think it might have been a city journalist I know. It's fascinating that Devereux would go to all the trouble of breaking in and rifling the place." He briefly described what he had found in the house.

"Oh, I don't know, all that prize money might be worth quite a bit of trouble to any number of us," Julia said. "But I'm afraid this is the end of *my* efforts. I've got to be back in London in the morning."

"Wasn't it kind of Julia to come down?" Lettie said. "She was an invaluable help keeping Nordstromson out of the way while I surveyed the ground between the site and the river."

"I did play up to him rather convincingly, don't you think?" Julia innocently asked, making J.D. squirm.

"You certainly had *me* fooled," he finally muttered. What a prize ass he'd been on her account! From here on in he'd play it cool. "Is there any hope of you doing one more favour for us when you get back to the city? I've got something that needs translating." He showed them the cassette box and a handful of papers. "All I could purloin from Nordstromson. Wish I hadn't been so rudely interrupted or I'd have made off with the cassette itself, and the map."

"Who interrupted you?"

He thought it had sounded like an army invasion.

"I don't know Swedish," Lettie said, gloating elatedly over the clues. "But this is one of those self-mailer containers, already labeled. Odd that it's—"

"Addressed to Finland, not Sweden?" J.D. supplied. "Finland is notably chummy with its Russian neighbours."

"Do you mean you think Nordstromson's a Russian spy?" Lettie asked, which got an incredulous hoot from Julia.

"It's not so crazy a notion," J.D. protested. "It would explain why his professional bona fides don't check out. And they don't. I'll wager there are projects at the Salisbury military preserve that the Russians would love to know about."

"Let's pretend for a moment that he *is* a Pinko

97

spy. Where does that lead? A Communist plot to steal Stonehenge? What for?" Julia argued.

"Ransom," J.D. suggested.

"A diversion," Lettie added, looking very thoughtful.

"Let's leave that question for the moment. What do you make of this?" He handed them one of the papers he'd stolen. "This is from a stack of identical copies on Nordstromson's desk. Note the symbol on the bottom, the international Ban the Bomb logo."

"An antinuclear activist! Yes, that seems more likely than a Soviet spy," nodded Julia.

"He could be a Red agent posing as an anti-nukey," J.D. countered.

"Or a red herring," Lettie added. It was a joke that set the pistons pumping in J.D.'s brain. He dropped his cigarette butt in an old milk bottle on the floor and began fiddling with brochures, constructing a three-sided structure while mumbling the words "Red Blinder."

Before they had a chance to ask him what he was up to there was a knock at the door. J.D. snapped his fingers and looked at his watch.

"It's nobody important, just a man who's come all the way from London to try to sell me a seaplane."

Saying good-bye, the women passed a slick young man on the doorstep. He was clutching an expensive briefcase in one hand and a model airplane in the other. The ever-hopeful salesman's look was rapidly evaporating as he took in the modest surroundings.

9

JOHN DAVID LEANED HIS LANKY BODY against the wall and gazed through the window at Lettie establishing herself inside the train. She settled in quickly, having only one piece of light hand luggage and a knitting bag. He chewed his lip and looked unhappy, wishing that he'd succeeded in discouraging her from going on this wild mission to infiltrate the Druids.

He was dubious, while she was convinced, that the false beard found in the canal linked the Druids to the crime. First of all, she'd argued, didn't the Druids claim that their ancient ancestors had built Stonehenge? Hadn't they protested when the fence went up to prevent public access? Although heartily agreeing that vandals should be prevented from continuing to despoil the sacred stones, they had insisted that religious freedom dictated their group's right to continue holding ceremonies in their holy place.

"But I thought Nordstromson said the Druids really had nothing to do with building Stonehenge," J.D. had objected.

"Archaeological evidence is completely against

their claim to it, but since the seventeenth century the general public has believed the monument was built by Druids. It takes more than a few years of science to obliterate three hundred years of humbug."

"So what does a false beard have to do with it?"

"It's been the Druid trademark for hundreds of years. They wear them at their ceremonies. Don't you understand, I've got to see where this clue leads."

He finally agreed. "Meanwhile I'll concentrate on the mechanical details. If we can discover *how*, it might lead us to *who*."

Lettie settled into her seat and waved out the window of the train at him. She had already grown quite fond of the fellow—even though he was slightly unscrupulous and devil-may-care. But what could one expect from a newspaperman? She mustn't let him see how worried she was about the case—he was so counting on the reward money! A young woman in a lavender raincoat turned and gave J.D. the up and down. There was no doubt that he had a certain unkempt sex appeal, but anyone could see that he would make a terrible husband, unless one thrived on clutter and insecurity.

For a while Lettie was too lost in thought to notice her fellow passengers. Or more accurately, lost in worry. She could easily imagine J.D. blundering into more trouble without her around to look after him. This concern for his safety had made her decision to go off to investigate the Druids a difficult one. But she had felt all along that they had something to do with the affair: it had a logic that appealed to her writer's instincts.

At this stage of her wool gathering she happened to hear "Stonehenge" spoken aloud, making her instantly aware of the conversation going on around her. Sitting beside her was a fat, swarthy man wearing a red fez and an ill-fitting brown serge suit. His hands, encrusted with rings, were twitching restlessly on his newspaper like bejeweled spiders doing the flamenco.

"So what ees theese Stonehinge that they make all the fuss?" he was asking of the thin-lipped cleric sitting across from him; a sour pickle, Lettie thought.

"A monumental loss, a monumental loss!" the man of God repeated in regretful tones. "It was the most excellent example of megalithic architecture in Britain—or all of Europe!"

"It's a scandal!" Lettie chimed in, taking her cue from the pointed look he gave her, then inquired if he was interested in ancient history.

"I wish I'd had the time to study it; I'm certain it must be fascinating," the clergyman replied.

"Like the Druids; I've always thought they were interesting," she sighed, and then confessed, "but I've never quite gotten it clear exactly who they were." Which was a lie, of course, like so much polite conversation.

"They were ancient Celtic sages and healers," the cleric explained. "They believed in love and brotherhood, just as we Christians do."

"The devil they did!" the sailor beside him interjected. "I read a book about them when I was at school. They were headhunters, specialising in human sacrifice." He let out a bloodthirsty laugh, patently for the benefit of the fair-haired girl across the aisle, who had been studiously avoiding looking in his direction. "They'd get stoned on too much wine and go have orgies under the moon. It was part of their worship. Sounds bloody marvelous, if you ask me." This produced an even more elaborate non-response from the object of his interest, but the man of the cloth made several heated remarks regarding youth's unhealthy preoccupation with hedonism.

"Although we'll probably never know what the ancient Druids were really like," Lettie calmly returned to the subject, hoping to smooth things over, "I'm sure that modern day Druids are perfectly decent, mostly charitable organisations. Winston Churchill joined the Albion Lodge of the Ancient Order of Druids in 1908."

"Indeed? I wasn't aware of that, but I'm quite certain that Churchill would never have joined any organisation that wasn't strictly above board," the man of God declared, obviously pleased to have expressed this sentiment.

"What about those crazies who are living like savages out in the woods?" the sailor challenged. "I read all about them in the papers. You can't tell me there isn't group nudity there, and *they* call themselves Druids."

The swarthy man in the fez looked amazed. Nudity! Not the English! And in such a cold climate! He would never understand them, even if he remained in this peculiar country for the rest of his life, Allah forbid.

"Young man, if you haven't anything but rude comments, I advise you to find a seat elsewhere." The vicar's tone was icy. The sailor took one last look at his fair, elusive prey, and seeing no joy there, slunk off in search of another seat near a more receptive female.

"Wayward youth!" The cleric's face pinched into a grimace.

"I believe he was purposely baiting you!"

"No respect for hees elders!" the man in the fez declared in a disgusted voice.

The train soon stopped and Lettie's fellow travellers got off. She stared out the window at the changing scenery and wondered what she would find when she reached her destination. It was just like one of those science-fiction stories that Julia enjoyed—here she was taking a train back in time, back to the Iron Age. She was on her way to try to join the very "group of crazies" the sailor had mentioned. "The Enlightened Order of the Iron Grove" was what they called themselves, a recent organisation of self-styled Druids endeavouring to grub out an authentically Iron-Aged existence back in the woods. She didn't *think* nudity would be a problem this time of year. Or at least she hoped not, never having been keen on that sort of thing.

She lapsed into another brown study on time. How peculiarly attractive the past was! No wonder folklore about Druids held such fascination! And the present seemed sadly deficient in magic for most of us, except for the scientists—their work kept them in constant touch with mystery. But didn't the masses working at humdrum jobs long for a little supernatural spice now and again? It wasn't too surprising that, from time to time, a few members of The Great Television Audience would drop out in favour of witchcraft, devil worship, or Druidism.

The train stopped at another station. A great crush of urban English streamed into the car until all the seats were filled. Lettie regarded them in their uniform ordinariness and wondered if they were happy. Just before the doors closed a noisy crowd of adolescents pushed on and stood by the door in a raucous mob. Crude, dirty thirteen-year-olds in combat boots and grubby jeans. Pimples and badly formed faces all crowded around one girl, trying to impress her with their tough posturing. She looked completely out of place among them—a vision of loveliness from a previous century. Long, wavy chestnut hair, roses in her cheeks, brown velvet eyes—a Constable shepherdess chewing gum, dressed in overalls and T-shirt. History had a way of refusing to stay in the past: an eighteenth-century garden beside a petrol station. Lettie sighed and shook her head, returning to the task of mentally preparing herself for the challenges of the Iron Age. Of course, there were other Druid sects to investigate if the first turned out to be blameless. She'd chosen to start with this one because an old acquaintance belonged to it. She would breathe easier once Natalie was proved innocent.

It was quite a hike back on a muddy track to the Iron Grove's settlement. Fortunately the day was fine, with no threat of rain. The snow lay in ever-shrinking patches under the bare clutter of chestnut and oak that rimmed the lane. As she ambled along, she took her mind off her aching leg muscles by thinking about Natalie.

It had been several years since Lettie had seen her. Natalie and Julia were old school chums, although they'd grown apart in adulthood, as Lettie had expected. Natalie had become even more serious and intellectual, while Julia had eventually got bored with it all, maturing into a wry, breezy connoisseur of lowbrow amusements. Natalie studied weaving, the lute, psychology, and any other Significant Subject her friends were discussing at the moment. Somehow her pale, thin face always looked slightly depressed, even when revelling in the "psychological resonances of basic human activities," her favorite topic at wine tasting parties.

About a year ago, after five years of union, Natalie came home early one night from her Woman's Ways symposium to find her husband in bed with her yoga teacher. The experience was so shattering that she left the next morning and joined the Druids. She had been dwelling in the Sacred Grove ever since, pretty much incommunicado with friends of her former life.

The first sign of the settlement was the point of a conically shaped thatched roof rising among the treetops. A little further along Lettie smelled woodsmoke and caught sight of the low mud wall that defined the compound and kept the cattle from wandering. She pushed open the gate and almost slipped in the foot of muck that covered the yard. Two long-haired men dressed in rough, woolen shirts, leather vests, and loose trousers had their backs to her as they chopped wood and loaded it onto a crude wooden sled. Nearby a woman was bending down to haul a bucket from the well. A black mongrel dog spotted the intruder and barked a warning, running towards her, teeth bared and tail wagging. The three stopped their work and turned to gape. Quelling an absurd fluttering in her stomach, Lettie met their unfriendly stares with a sunny, "Hullo! I do hope I've come to the right place. I'm a friend of Natalie Fisher's."

This information broke the spell. "Yes, Natalie lives here." The young woman nodded, her long black braids flapping against the front of her ankle-length, shapeless dress. She had one of those fresh-scrubbed, glowing-with-health faces. "I'll go find her for you," she promised, disappearing into the round house, which was the largest building in the compound. It had only a few narrow windows and a door to break up its squat mud walls. The most dramatic feature of the structure was its high roof, which Lettie thought rather beautiful.

Without a word, the men resumed their chopping. A rooster came strutting out of one of the lean-tos and flew up on the wall, perching among the carved wooden heads mounted there. Each had a frowning gargoyle's face turned to the outside and a smiling face turned inwards. Lettie knew she had seen heads like these in books on Celtic art— they were supposed to frighten off the evil spirits without and bless the inhabitants within.

Pushing aside the goat skin that hung over the door, the woman reemerged with a familiar round-shouldered figure behind her. "Why, it's Lettie Win-terbottom!" Natalie cried, surprised but pleased to see her. "What brings you all the way out here?" Even while smiling she managed to look her usual glum self, but with marked improvements. Her mass of wiry brown hair made an attractively messy halo around her face—much more flattering than that severe pinned-back look she'd always affected. Her complexion looked healthy, and she'd trimmed down a bit.

"Natalie, dear! How well you look!" Lettie sang out, grasping both the woman's hands.

"Thank you! And so do you!"

"A vision brought me to your door." Lettie's voice had suddenly acquired a solemn hush.

"Really!" Natalie looked slightly taken aback. "I wasn't aware that you had visions."

"Well I don't usually. That's what made this one all the more. . ." She fluttered her hands in an inarticulate gesture before getting on with it. "I was sitting by the fire, knitting and watching the telly, when the picture began to flicker. I rubbed my eyes, thinking it might be eyestrain, and looked again. There on the screen—where only seconds before had been Mrs. Woodhouse teaching an unruly bulldog's owner how to make him go walkies—was a group of old men in white robes and long grey beards. They were whispering among themselves in a language I couldn't understand. As if that weren't quite enough, I was no longer alone! A young man was sitting beside me, also watching the telly. He put a finger to the side of his nose and asked, 'How is Natalie?'"

"Extraordinary!" Natalie gasped. "I don't suppose this was on a Thursday? It was a few Thursdays ago that I suddenly thought of you."

"I believe it was a Thursday!" Lettie replied. "I woke up later. The fire had gone out, the television station was off for the night. There was no sign of the young man. I suppose it might have been a dream, but it left me with an undeniable urge to come see you—just to be assured that all is well."

"That's very kind of you, but I'm quite happy here," she declared, making an all-embracing gesture of their rough camp. Lettie found it oddly touching to see this closed-up creature make such an expansive movement.

"I'm so glad! You understand that the old bearded men in my vision were Druids."

"And the young man who asked about me—it wasn't . . . John?" She said her ex-husband's name reluctantly, as if it were a four-letter word.

"Oh, no, it was my banker. I feel very strongly that the whole experience was directing me here—to you and the Druids. I interpret my banker's role in the affair as an indication that I ought to make a monetary contribution to your cause. For weeks I have been unable to shake a terrible sense of restlessness and dissatisfaction. Time for a change . . . and here I am!"

Natalie wiped away a stray lock of hair and stared disbelievingly into Lettie's angelic blue eyes. "Then you've come to join us?"

"Well . . . I suppose I have!" was Lettie's amazed response, as if she'd only just understood it herself.

Hilsebeck groaned aloud as he drove towards Portsmouth's waterfront. This Druid business was just too far out; why Lettie was so keen on it was completely beyond him. But by the time he'd located a certain Captain Tree's Salvage, he was beginning to have second thoughts. If it turned out that ransom wasn't the motive—who else but a cult of weirdos would have the motivation required to commit such an absurd and grandiose offense?

Captain Herbert Tree certainly looked the part. He was short, his portly build nicely set off by a fine, well-trimmed beard. He wore a faded captain's hat, a rolled-neck sweater, thick khaki trousers, and rubber knee boots. He smoked a crooked briar pipe, which made him look even more like an advertisement for men's cologne. His first question, after shaking hands with Hilsebeck, seemed to reinforce the impression that here was somebody who didn't mind looking the part. "I say, where's your photographer?"

The reporter obligingly brought out the staff camera, a fully automatic model, since J.D. had never advanced beyond the point-and-shoot school of photography. Captain Tree looked dissatisfied; he'd obviously expected an extra chap sporting a folded-up hat brim who would be constantly squeezing off rapid-fire shots with an enormous press camera.

A light rain was falling outside, beating softly on the tin roof high over their heads. The home of Tree's Salvage was an enormous old warehouse, inadequately lit by occasional lights hanging from the rafters. There were innumerable dark corners as well as sinister house-sized pieces of machinery: donkey engines, reels of cable, a diving bathyscaphe. They wandered through the corridors created haphazardly between the clutter of equipment. The overall odour of the place was a mixture of grease and sea salt, accented by the metallic taste of rust in one's mouth.

"Here's a likely spot," Tree said, cutting short his own monologue about machinery. It hadn't taken more than a word to get him going.

"Hmm?" J.D. had only been half listening, one ear peeled for any useful facts.

"For the photos, lad." He straightened his cap and clenched his pipe between his teeth, posing in front of a collection of diving suits hung on pegs against one wall. The row of brass helmets, battered and scarred by years of sub-oceanic use, were nearly on the same level as the captain's head. Even to Hilsebeck's untrained eye, it looked ludicrous: an underwater class photo. But knowing that Tree was the only man in the world who could guide him back out of this maze, he attached the flash to the camera and clicked away. Afterwards, Tree heartily slapped him on the back, then threw open a door that had been just out of sight in the shadows. J.D. squinted as daylight poured in from outside. "Come on, laddie, the interestin' things are out here in the yard." Stumbling over the sill, the journalist followed.

Ahead of him, the captain strode out onto a stone jetty; here everything was more neatly organised than inside. There were coils of rubber hose, pallet-mounted compressors, huge woven metal slings expansive enough to wrap round the bottom of a ship. It all was built to gargantuan scale, and made J.D. feel like a mouse creeping into a workshop.

Captain Tree patted an accordioned rubber bladder fondly. The row of wrinkled black objects extended down to the end of the pier; there must have been at least forty of them. "These are what you asked about on the phone. Caissons, we call 'em. They look like giant balloons when inflated."

"And this is the associated equipment?"

"Some of it. You've got yer compressors, here." He hooked a thumb at the appropriate gadget, looking like something out of a giant refrigerator. "Couple on the hose, drop 'em over the side, then inflate the caissons. Got to be done at the face of the wreck, mind you."

"Sounds straightforward enough," J.D. commented, taking a few more pictures, being careful to include the captain in most.

"Straightforward! Great Scott! It's an art, laddie. An art!"

Sensing the beginning of a long, salty tale, J.D. prompted, "So where does the art come in?"

Captain Tree spat in disgust at landlubbers everywhere. "Take a simple weld. You're at four hundred feet depth, breathin' nitrogen so pure you quack like Donald Duck. You've got fifteen minutes to do your job before you begin to black out from the cold and pressure. It's like tryin' to walk through Yorkshire puddin' down there, and the visibility's about the bloody same. You try and lay down a weld—a job you could do in two minutes topside takes five times as long. You pray the narcosis don't spoil your aim. If that torch burns your glove, you'll implode into yer helmet." He paused to suck furiously on his pipe, noticed that it had gone out, and applied a match to it. Despite Hilsebeck's innate skepticism, he had to admit the old seadog could transform the details of marine engineering difficulties into a colourful tale.

The captain smiled triumphantly. "And that's

111

just one little bit of detail work. When it's ready to rise, you've got to get the balance right; we use what's called a manifold up on the salvage ship. I do that myself. It's a big network of valves, like a giant calliope, each feedin' a caisson. That's how you bleed air out or add it in. You need all the lift you can get to break the bottom suction. But when she's loose, it's Katie bar the door! That wreck will come up like an express lift!"

"Right under you?"

"I should damned well hope not!" Tree cried. "We stand off to one side; the hoses all lead out to a sort of raft. That's where the art is, you see; you have to bleed air out quick enough to slow the ascent. But you've got to keep it balanced and level."

J.D.'s head was starting to spin with all this data. He'd been under the impression that they just pumped everything full and it came to the surface like a rubber duckie. "Sounds like playing with a runaway freight train."

"Worse!"

"But being inland, our readers would probably be interested in how salvage is done in rivers," J.D. suggested slyly.

"Salvage of what, exactly?" Tree asked, with obvious contempt for anything smaller than the *Lusitania*.

"Pleasure craft, barges. How would one raise a barge weighing . . . oh, forty tons or so?"

The captain couldn't disguise his scorn. "You're talkin' about toy boats! My equipment alone weighs ten times that!"

"But supposing you wanted to raise forty tons."

"Well, you'd use a derrick barge and just lift

up. . . ." He rubbed his handsome moustache and thought for a moment before adding, "But on a river you might not have the room. It'd be like a giant tryin' to get dressed in a suitcase."

"Couldn't you use caissons like these?"

"Not these. You're lookin' at four hundred tons of lift here. They'd float your boat right up over the trees!"

"Surely there are smaller bladders?"

"Follow me." He set off down the centre of the dock, rummaging around, looking under tarps, kicking aside crates of valves and fittings. "Here we be!" He pointed at last to a much smaller caisson; deflated it was a little larger than a steamer trunk. "We use these little blighters for balance. They're small enough to stick inside the wreck, and then inflate."

"What would this one lift?"

"It'll do forty tons, nice enough. Not by itself, though."

"Why not?"

"Balance, for starters. With a single unit, you'd only get one end out of the water. It would take two, and four would be better yet. Even with two you can get the damndest yaw."

"Oh yes. . . ."

"That side to side rockin' is murder. Get them out of balance, too much lift on one side, and it starts gettin' worse and worse." Tree made a seesaw gesture with his hands.

"Creating a nasty situation."

"Doesn't it just! I've seen 'em turn big ships into turtles. And with all the excess lift on a forty-ton vessel, you'd have to be bloody careful, and standin' well off to one side. Even a little wreck like you're talkin' about could smash you into mincemeat."

J.D.'s ears perked up. An accurate description of the state of the corpse in the canal. Could an expert handler of the valves use it as an instrument of murder? "How would you attach these devices?"

"With a sling cradle, I'd say." Captain Tree sounded impatient. "I thought your readers wanted some real dramatic tales of the sea."

"Who knows what readers want? We got a lot of nice comments on our series on repotting perennials."

J.D. didn't notice the determined look in the captain's eye as he steered him by the elbow. "Come on into my cabin, mate. We'll have a rum together." J.D. nodded, his head full of how neat and simple it must have been: rope on the bladders, float the short distance into the canal, then let the air out. Everything settles to the bottom safely out of sight until the weather permits raising them up and taking them out to sea.

Now if only he could discover how they had got the stones down *to* the Avon. He returned to the present to find a glass of dark rum in his hand and the expansive Captain Tree sailing full force into a salty tale. "There I was, two hundred feet down, the whole weight of the wreck on top of me, ooze at my back, my hoses wrapped around my legs. And then, in the little circle of light from my headlamp, I saw. . ."

10

THE HUNTING PARTY RETURNED—a ragged, hairy bunch looking exhausted and very dirty. Rabbits and rats were strung over their backs, caught with the help of snares and tamed ferrets, which they carried in woven cages. There was much talk of adventure as they scrubbed their hands and faces with chunks of yellow homemade soap. In spite of the confusion, they all noticed the unexpected stranger. Her well-tailored purple winter coat and gay red hat and mittens didn't blend in too well with their cruder homespun. There were raised eyebrows and muttered "Who's this?" Lettie chuckled to herself, knowing how funny the scene would appear from a distance—a shaggy horde of Celts milling about, giving the meticulously-groomed invader from the twentieth century a wide berth.

They thronged into the house, leaving her alone outside. The louder snatches of discussion drifted out as they tried to decide what to do about her. She drooped onto a log and hoped they wouldn't vote to send her off this late in the day. It was a three-mile trek out to the highway and a long wait for a coach into town. She sighed, unable to suppress a longing for her easy chair and a nice hot cup of tea. Then Natalie's face appeared at the door, calling, "Come in and have a nice hot cup of blood pudding with us." Swallowing her repugnance, Lettie sprang up to accept the invitation. Blood pudding notwithstanding, it was a foot in the door.

Although Lettie would probably be turfed out once their leader, the Most Enlightened One, put in his appearance, Natalie dutifully prepared her for initiation. This consisted of vague references to how dreadful the rites were, while they spent the next morning trekking through the woods looking for the right kind of materials for basketweaving. Of course there was no sign of Stonehenge, but they wouldn't exactly flaunt it to some outsider.

Far and away the most intriguing Druid, the one Lettie was anxious to meet, was the enigmatic Most Enlightened One. They said his actual identity was unknown. No one had even seen his face—he always wore a mask in their presence. Their voices acquired a hushed quality when they spoke of him. Whatever manner of beast he was, he certainly had to have charisma.

"What's he like?" Lettie asked while helping to prepare a stew that afternoon.

"Wonderful and terrible," said Natalie.

"Fierce and loving," someone else said. The adjectives flew thick and fast.

"He's like I always expected Jesus Christ to be," one woman sighed, her face alight with devotion, "only better looking."

"My!" Lettie exclaimed. "He does sound like

something special! But how do you know he's good-looking? I thought he always wore a mask."

"She means his body," Natalie patiently explained, peeling a carrot.

"Should I dice a few more turnips?" Lettie asked, to cover her embarrassment.

That evening, dinner was a festive affair. A yeasty mead was passed around, and everyone was in high spirits. When the food was consumed and the dishes washed, Natalie asked Lettie to go into her room and close the door, explaining, "We must prepare for our celebration. When the house grows quiet you may come sit here by the fire. We will be out under the Sacred Oaks waiting to greet the Most Enlightened One. He will be here soon."

"What if he doesn't come?" Lettie asked, thinking of the man who had died in the canal. "Surely you won't wait all night?"

"If need be."

"But how will you keep warm?"

"We will keep a fire going. You must not follow us. We are all sworn to protect our secrets, at any cost."

"Don't worry!" Lettie said, hiding her annoyance at the implicit threat. "I don't intend to blunder around alone in the dark and risk a broken ankle."

The night passed slowly as agitation was eventually replaced by resignation. There was nothing for it but to sit by the fire spinning wool and trying to calm down. Lettie worked until her eyes ached, then despondently went to bed.

The next thing she knew there was a tap at her door. "Wake up." It was Natalie's voice. "The sun's rising. We must be off."

"Where to?" Lettie asked groggily, rolling over and groping for her clothes in the twilight.

"To look for mistletoe. I have a basket of food; we'll eat on the way."

It had to be significant that they were going to look for the Druids' sacred plant. "Does this mean he arrived last night?" she asked, pushing open the screen that served as a door. Poor Natalie was hollow-eyed with a little smear of green on her cheek that looked like paint. There was a smudge of red on her chin. Lettie hoped that was also paint.

"I'll tell you as we walk."

Lettie wondered about this sudden show of impatience as she allowed herself to be ushered out of the empty house and into the wood. There was no sign of any of the group going about their usual morning chores. "Where is everyone?"

"Hiding," her guide replied, taking the left fork that curved away from the camp and deep into the wilderness. "You must see no one today but me, your teacher."

"Then the Most Enlightened One is willing. . ."

"Yes. I put your petition before him, and he has seen fit to give you a chance to prove yourself worthy."

"How do I do that?"

"Tonight he will ask you sacred questions. You will have memorised the sacred answers. Then he will ask one final question that you must answer directly from your heart. If your answer pleases him he will allow you to continue the initiation. After that it gets pretty awful, but no one can prepare you for that part." She turned to Lettie with a terrible gravity only Natalie could manage. "It is an ordeal worse than you can imagine! I wish you'd change your mind and go back to St. Martin's Mere where you belong!"

"I'm afraid I'd feel terribly let down."

"Very well. Your first answer will be. . ."

The sun was setting when Natalie pointed out a lightning-blasted stump, a landmark near the camp. As they got closer Lettie felt her weariness being supplanted by a sensation akin to stage fright. Her first initiation rite! What would the vicar at home have to say if he could see her now!

"Here we are," Natalie was saying, pointing towards a stone circle that was much smaller and not half so impressive as Stonehenge. "Walk into the centre and sit on the sacrificial stone. Hold the mistletoe in your right hand and speak to no one until you hear the voice of the Most Enlightened One, then give your answers." With that she dashed away down the path towards the house, leaving Lettie quite alone.

Lettie sat for what seemed like hours, just watching the sky change from violet to blue to black. An owl hooted. The wind made the branches squeak and whine. A creature rustled in the thicket. The cold crept into her bones and made her shiver, which didn't contribute to her attempts at detachment. "It might be my funeral," she said aloud, "but I intend to enjoy the service."

There was a muffled footfall, then an approaching light. A ghostly figure glided into the circle and stooped to drop his burden of kindling, piling it up, and setting it ablaze with his lantern's flame. He was dressed in a flowing sleeveless garment decorated with teeth and feathers. He uttered no sound and as soon as the fire was going stepped back and took his place in front of the stones. Another figure appeared, also in white, wearing a fox's pelt for a hat. The animal's dead, staring face hung down over the Druidess' forehead, the rest of the skin covered her hair and shoulders. Her face and arms were painted white. She added more wood to the fire and stood silently beside her brother. Soon everyone was there, forming a column of white inside the circle.

Something black flapped by her head. Lettie swallowed a scream and ducked; she had never been fond of bats. A flute began to trill a slow, sad tune, punctuated by a soft drum beat.

The chorus started to chant:

"Oh spirit of the Ancient One,
Come walk in that new world which is so old,
Come speak to us, O Shadow of the Owls! . . ."

A deep, resonant voice answered from the enclosure behind the stone archway:

"I, the Wind of the Western Sea,
Sense a strange wind
Moving among the Sacred Oaks."

Startled, Lettie recognised her cue and heard herself quavering:

"What great thing knows a hedgehog?
I would know it too."

The Most Enlightened One replied:

"It is a thing you know now,
Yet must always search for."

The flute stopped. The drum picked up its tempo. A female began to weep softly.

Most Enlightened One:

> *"What is the mistletoe?*
> *Is it a bush or a tree?"*

Lettie:

> *"Neither. It is today—*
> *That which never was,*
> *And never shall be,*
> *Yet is."*

The chorus began to gently sway to the beat of the drum. The head Druid's voice thundered:

> *"I am brother to dragons and companion to owls*
> *I am the boot that walks without a foot,*
> *A goat of many colours.*
> *Dare you approach and stand before me,*
>   *Stranger?"*

Lettie answered:

> *"They call you terrible and gentle."*

The Most Enlightened One:

> *"Brothers and Sisters of the Sacred Grove,*
> *Bring me the Stranger so that I may know her."*

Two of the chorus stepped forward, one on either side of Lettie. Taking her arms, they ushered her through the archway into the small, shadowy enclosure just behind the circle. Here there was only a faint glow from the fire. The rest of the chorus was now out of sight, a good ten paces away. She could barely make out a dark figure seated cross-legged atop a stone. He was wearing some kind of animal mask—only his eyes and fangs gleamed in the gloom; the rest was indistinguishable. They let go of her arm and left the antechamber, returning to their places among the group that remained outside.

The Most Enlightened One's voice softened slightly, since she was now only a few feet from him:

"Have you seen three rooks in the naked larch?
Have you brought back a souvenir from Atlantis?
Do the Polynesians know your name?
Speak to me of your vision."

Lettie hesitated, trying to recall the right answer, but the memorised responses had run out. She would have to come up with something of her own. She groped frantically for just the right wording for her make-believe vision; some way to make it fit into this peculiar potluck of phrases from the poets and the Scriptures. . . . Ah! That was it!

"Yes, I have had a vision;
Of old men scheming schemes,
And young men seeing television."

Her reply was slightly tinged with pride at her own wit under fire. Then the shadowy Druid bubbled over with laughter—a remarkable laugh full of mirth. Lettie realised, with a shock, that she'd heard it before. The background drum abruptly stopped. There was a faint gasp from the chorus as someone whispered, "No one has ever heard him laugh!" To which came Lettie's sotto voce response that only the Most Enlightened One could hear:

"Nonsense! Millions have heard him laugh, and his laugh is worth millions!"

Now it was time for the Enlightened One to gasp, and finally reply in a very low voice that didn't carry beyond the antechamber: "You have an extraordinary ear."

Lettie whispered, "And you have an extraordinary laugh—instantly recognisable! Tell me, how would your followers feel if they knew you played Dinky the Clown in the adverts for the Dinky Burger chain? And what would the Dinky Burger executives say if the press were to reveal the offbeat manner in which you spend your weekends? Hardly the sort of wholesome stuff the kiddies have come to expect from Dinky the Clown."

"Dammit! I need that job until my car's paid off!" His voice was still low, but barely controlled. "All right, you've got me by the short and curlies! What the devil do you want? You're not one of those damned investigative reporters, are you?"

"An eye for an eye, a truth for a truth," she couldn't resist quipping. It was turning into quite an amusing party.

"Fair enough. You keep my secret and I owe you a favour."

"Agreed. Where is Stonehenge?"

"I wish I knew! I could use the money. . . . So *that's* what you're up to!" he muttered, some of the tension leaving his voice. "I've got an alibi for that, you know. I was stranded at the television studio for three days—couldn't even get back to my flat. I've got at least a dozen witnesses."

"What about your group here? Nothing but mutual alibis for them, I suppose?"

"Of course . . . what do you expect? They never leave these woods; it's against the rules. And even if they left, how would they move those stones with a handful of people and some crude tools?"

It was a point well taken, and she said as much. "One more question. Do you use those long grey false beards in your ceremonies? You know, like the ones in all the old pictures of Druids."

"That tired stuff?" He snickered derisively. "We are strictly into face and body paint, tattoos, and animal pelts. No false beards."

"What about the other Druid organisations still extant? Are you in touch with them?"

"Not really. There's the Ancient Order of the Beneficent Druids; they're a bunch of old dearies who give money away to homes for wayward hamsters and the like. They don't even go in for any decent ceremony. The whole thing's a snore. Then there's the Sons and Daughters of the Golden Sickle— 'The New Grove,' for short. They're not much on prophetic truths, but very big on profit margins. I believe they sometimes sport false beards—maybe at their ritual counting of the Sacred Monthly Receipts. A big phony that calls himself the New Wizard runs the whole operation based on donating all your earthly goods and labour to the Faith. He's grown rich on that scam, with a following of several thousand brainwashed toadies, a couple of villas, and a fleet of Jaguars." A note of envy tinged the Most Enlightened One's voice.

"Where can I find this New Wizard?" she asked.

"He just built a concrete and glass monolith out near Heathrow."

"I see. Thank you very much, you've been most

helpful. Now why don't you yell out that you've
found me unworthy and that I'm to leave the
Grove after a good night's sleep."

The Most Enlightened One raised his voice so
that once again all could hear:

> "Brothers and Sisters of the Sacred Grove,
> I have looked into the Stranger,
> And found a mote.
> Let her sleep at our hearth,
> And depart with first morning's light.
> But she must swear to keep our secrets,
> Or her tongue will be cut out,
> And fed to the water voles!"

Then Lettie called out:

> "I will accept your wise judgement,
> Most Enlightened One,
> My lips are forever sealed.
> The water voles have no need,
> Of an old woman's tongue."

11

JENKS WAS LYING IN WAIT when Hilsebeck shambled into the office, late as usual. The editor pinned him against the coffee machine and demanded a progress report. "From the looks of your last two stories, you've been doing nothing but spinning your wheels."

"That's because I'm playing my cards close to my chest, Your Editorship. I won't show my aces until the prize money is safely in my pocket. Only then will I write the story of our brilliant detective work."

"Our?"

"Oh, didn't I tell you? I've got an assistant. She's doing an undercover investigation of the Druids. Meanwhile I'm trying to learn how the job was actually accomplished."

"That would make a corker—'The Impossible Crime, How It Was Done.' I like it . . . when can I have it?"

"Not until I clear up the particulars," J.D. said, explaining that the only bit left was how the stones were moved across the landscape without leaving tracks in the ground.

"I might know someone who would have some ideas on that," Jenks said and went away. He returned shortly with a satisfied gleam in his eye. "It's all arranged for this afternoon. Drive up to London and meet your contact at three o'clock by the *A* stacks in the reading room of the Science Museum. Know where that is?"

"Just around the corner from Hyde Park."

"That's it. In the meantime," Jenks added on his way out, "try and stay awake."

J.D. contemplated chucking out several days worth of paperwork along with a dozen almost empty plastic coffee cups that graced the mess on his desk. There was more paper here than substance, he thought as he doused a cigarette in cold brown sediment. But before he could begin tidying up someone tapped at his frosted glass door. As usual, J.D. didn't respond. It was part of a study he was doing on the English attitude towards closed office doors. The average person knocked, waited to be told to come in, then entered whether he was invited or not.

"I didn't say come in," J.D. said as Nemesis itself came strolling in. "You're invading my space."

Devereux smirked as he took in the cubbyhole of a nowhere newspaper's star reporter. "Don't tell me I'm interfering with your work?"

"I suppose one can't expect manners from a cat burglar," J.D. threw back in his most bored voice. It had no noticeable effect on the unwelcome guest, who was showing every sign of making himself at home in an unsteady folding chair.

"What's all that?" He nodded at a pile of papers J.D. was covering with his arms. "Ransom notes?"

"No, just the start of my existential novel."

Devereux pulled out a monogrammed cigarette case and offered its contents to his rival. "Smoke? Rather a nice blend. I've got a man who brings a few plugs in from the Balkans."

Up your Balkans, J.D. silently proposed as he accepted one of the black cigarettes, nearly choking on the first evil-smelling puff.

"Ransom is a damned good motive," his guest was saying. "Especially since those rocks have no intrinsic value. You might say I'm devoting most of my time to the ransom angle."

And getting nowhere, or you wouldn't be here, J.D. was tempted to reply, but only said, "You're fishing for something, no doubt?"

"Of course. Your connection with the local constabulary must be useful."

J.D. suppressed a snicker. If only Devereux knew how useless Coggs was to him! "What about those contacts with the CID that you're always bragging about? Not to mention your new army pals. You didn't waste any time siccing them on me at Nordstromson's the other night, did you?"

"I never thought I'd hear you sound so paranoid. Of course, you may have good reason. Is Miss Winterbottom back, by the way? How did she fare with the New Druids?"

"So you've been spying on your competition. What's the matter, no ideas of your own?"

"Listen, Hilsebeck, a commission is better than losing out all together. I'm offering you quid pro quo. You haven't a prayer of finding them the way you've been floundering around. And I'm prepared to make you an offer in exchange for information." He was obviously beginning to lose his temper.

"Your usual deal—you get the pie, I get the pie plate." The encounter was getting to J.D.'s coffee-edged nerves as well. In another moment he would grab this shifty little bastard by the collar and heave him out. But he shouldn't have put it off. In another moment Devereux was gone.

J.D. slouched back in his chair and wished he knew if Devereux really had any inside dope on ransoms. It cheered him to assume that Devereux was all wind. But he did know about Lettie and where she was. How was that?

Hilsebeck was almost to London before his vague feeling of discomfort crystallised into a conviction that he was being followed. He passed the rest of the drive trying to figure out who was after him, and considering ways to lose the nondescript grey Cortina that was always just a few car lengths back.

Once they got into heavy Kensington traffic, the Cortina was forced to follow closer, which suited J.D. just fine. He slammed on his brakes and swerved into a familiar garage, barely avoiding getting pranged by an oncoming car. He heard the squeal of brakes out on the street as he nipped behind a wide concrete pillar and stopped. The Cortina roared past, the driver evidently assuming that his quarry had gone up the spiral ramp to the upper levels. J.D. hadn't been able to see who it was.

J.D. backed out and proceeded up the ramp, taking the first available parking space. He'd alighted and was kneeling behind a limousine when the grey roof of the Cortina cruised by, then parked down the row.

Determined to identify his shadow, J.D. came out of hiding and walked quickly towards the Cortina, but its driver was gone, the door to the stairway swinging closed. J.D. walked around the car, trying the doors, but they were locked. It looked like a motor pool vehicle with a company sticker that said JETCO. So it wasn't one of Devereux's spies, anyway.

Aware that the Cortina's driver was still likely to be in the neighborhood, he took a number 28 bus down the High Street, braving the brisk air of the open upper deck. There was no sign of muscular KGB mugs with lethal umbrellas.

It felt comfortable to be jostling along the crowded sidewalks and inhaling diesel fumes again. He passed shops he used to browse through, and nodded to a familiar wrinkled face behind a magazine kiosk. No point in fooling himself; he missed his former London reporter days. The job had carried a certain hollow cachet good for a free drink or tickets to a new show. J.D. felt a twinge of alien emotion that could only be regret. It really had been a pleasant enough life, if one toed the line.

The museum entrance opened right into the natural history exhibit. He passed the innumerable glass cases of mollusks without a second glance. But he did pause to admire the jaw bone of a great white shark that loomed over the archway that went through to the technology section.

The rendezvous table was occupied by an intense-looking schoolboy. "Hilsebeck, I presume?" he inquired, setting aside a dog-eared copy of

Jane's *All the World's Aircraft.* "Please have a seat. I'm Stanley Jenks. Granddad told me about your problem."

The reporter nodded, momentarily taken aback by the spectacle of a Jenks progeny. The familial twitchy nose was there, but not much else. This Jenks looked about twelve years old. His most obvious physical attributes were large hands and feet dangling awkwardly from long limbs. He was waving about one of those overgrown appendages as he expounded. "I immediately concluded that the weather was the essential drawback, but in no way insurmountable. Consider conditions on the Alaskan pipeline."

"Only eliminate all roads and put a seventy-two-hour time limit on the whole operation."

"Precisely," the boy continued in the comfortable drone of a born lecturer. "But the critical factor was the snow pack itself. Thick enough to cover minor surface irregularities like stones and fallen limbs, but not deep enough to prevent heavy tread marks underneath. Therefore whatever carried away the monument was capable of passing lightly over the snow, or of not touching it at all." He smiled, daring his pupil to guess.

J.D. tried. "Balloons—no, that's silly, they'd never support that kind of weight. . . ." He snapped his fingers. "A hovercraft! Why didn't I think of that before?"

"No, a hovercraft would be too large to fit through the space between the trees that Grandfather mentioned. Also hovercraft are too noisy. Even the storm winds would not have covered the racket those engines make. And they would be difficult to hide or even transport without notice."

"Too bad, a hovercraft goes over snow like a dream."

"I know; in fact, it inspired me to see if there was any other device that operated upon similar principles, which brings me to this." He held up a copy of *Aviation Week,* folded back a page, and pushed it towards J.D., who quickly perused the article devoted to something called an airlift. It was a simple air cushion platform used to move around and install jet engines. The device consisted of a flat pallet with air jets underneath, and self-contained battery-powered motors to supply the lift. The photo showed one workman effortlessly pushing a thirty-ton engine.

J.D. took a deep breath and said that this sounded exactly right. He was afraid effusive praise might offend this one, so refrained from turning cartwheels.

"Yes, I know." Stanley smiled thinly. "Once tamped down with rollers, the snow would provide a perfect surface for the airlifts. It would be a piece of cake, providing they minded the basic laws of physics."

"Meaning inertia?"

"Mmm hmm. Forty tons in motion develops a hefty momentum. Steep declines would be hazardous."

"They avoided those, sure enough. Good gawd, Stanley, well done! I hope your grandfather explained why you've got to keep this under your hat."

"Of course you can rely on me completely," was the solemn reply.

"Excellent. Any idea who manufactures these airlifts in England?"

"No, sorry."

"Ever hear of JETCO?"

"They make the new Viper. You know, the cruise missile. They're one of those companies that were recently nationalized."

"Would JETCO have airlifts?"

"I can't imagine why. Cruise missiles have very small motors. But one of JETCO's subsidiaries might use airlifts for something."

"Good point." The newspaperman rose, eager to be testing the value of the gem this boy had just handed him. "Thank you again. You have been enormously helpful. If I get the brass ring, I shall see that you have a nice commission."

"That would be decent of you," Stanley said, excitement finally breaking through his facade of prodigal detachment. "If there's anything else I can do. . ."

"As a matter of fact, there is. You see, I'm being followed." J.D. was gratified that this announcement produced the classic Jenks gleam. "You wouldn't, by any chance, know of a back way out of here?"

Lettie and the Druids parted amicably with relieved smiles all around. It was a little disappointing that the Most Enlightened One didn't deign to make an appearance, but apparently he didn't go in much for daylight work. Lettie strolled out the lane with a light, easy step, watching the high flying clouds and feeling all was right with the world. She came away convinced that Natalie and her bunch, although dupes, were definitely not thieves.

Waiting for the coach to take her to the nearest train station, she considered her next move. It seemed pointless to investigate the Ancient Order of Beneficent Druids. She'd heard a bit about them and knew that the Most Enlightened One's description of them as just a charitable organization was accurate. The only group left to tackle was the New Grove, in all its high-tech spirituality.

The New Grove's recently built facility near Heathrow Airport was a three-storied modern affair with masses of concrete ominously overhanging the walkways from the car park.

Lettie went through the swinging doors into an impressive high-ceilinged lobby done in rosy Italian marble and illuminated by a pyramid-shaped skylight. It was incongruously decorated with macrame hangings and a healthy grove of young oaks in concrete pots. There was a sickle-shaped pool inhabited by fat domesticated trout dreaming in the shade of the potted forest. A waterfall splashed out of a tube in the wall, creating a background of cheery clatter echoing through the lobby.

Lettie approached the business end—a high counter that ran the entire length of one side of the room. There were three neat, smiling young people in green smocks standing behind the counter, all looking terribly anxious to ensure that she had a nice day.

Lettie greeted them politely, looking from one

beaming face to the next: one male, two female, all sugar-coated.

"Yes? How can we assist you?" the peppy little blonde asked as all three leaned eagerly across the counter.

"I am planning to open a chain of boutiques— one in the Canaries, two on Capri, three in Rome, and one in the Poconos." She paused and the trio percolated with encouragement. "So I am here to research what merchandise is available. But not just anything will do. I want knickknacks that resonate back through human history. In short, knickknacks with a message."

She had said the magic word. They began to effervesce, and in a twinkling were giving her a tour of "the plant," as they called it. "In the organic sense, as well as the industrial," explained the bubbling brunette, "we are all leaves of the same tree, with our roots in the primeval soil of history."

"Then show me your fruit," Lettie said, well aware that it was a lame little witticism. As the three hooted ecstatically Lettie couldn't help but nurture a tiny acorn of disdain.

They first took her into a showroom where all their Druid products were attractively displayed under spotlights. They manufactured an amazing variety of merchandise: Druid dolls and puppets, mugs, ashtrays, a cookery book entitled *Ancient Celtic One-Pot Dishes,* sex aids, golf club mittens, diet books, calendars, key fobs, body musk, and Loincloth Brand knickers that looked like real badger fur—"They're Reversible!" the package said.

"And we're considering getting into designer jeans," remarked one of her guides.

"But we hear the market's pretty tight," the brunette delivered the punch line, producing another explosion of ecstatic hoots.

"Next we'll show you our manufacturing area," the blonde told her when the laughter had subsided.

Lettie hesitated, feeling weak with apprehension of what she might see there. Would there be bays full of modern manufacturing equipment operated by wild-looking Druids in animal skins? Would they be wearing the standard yellow plastic safety hats— or Viking helmets replete with horns? The anticipation made her slightly giddy.

Fortunately, reality proved much tamer: long rooms where hundreds of smiling Druids, all dressed in green smocks and trousers, were pasting Druid decals on white mugs imported from Korea.

"Our net profits were muscular last year!" she was told.

"At the start of the next fiscal year there will be a new stock issue; our dividends should double."

She managed to escape their pitch temporarily by backing through a door marked LADIES. For a moment she was afraid that the females would follow, still chattering away about profit profiles, but they remained outside, taking advantage of her absence to hold an impromptu sales meeting.

But the lavatory was not completely empty. Leaning against the basin, crying at her reflection in the mirror, was a slim freckle-faced woman of about twenty. Although wearing the official green smock, she was exhibiting conspicuously unDruidlike behaviour. Hers was the first unsmiling face Lettie had seen since she'd entered the building.

The young woman took one look at Lettie's grandmotherly demeanor and threw her arms around her neck. Lettie patted the quaking shoulders and cooed, "There, there! What is it child?"

"It's my Brian! They all tell me that he's been deprogrammed and there's nothing to be done about it. I'm out of my head with worry!" She lapsed into heartrending sobs and hiccuping.

"Try to take it a step at a time. Where is Brian now?"

"I don't know! He's been gone for five days! He never would have left for that long without telling me!"

"And who says he's been deprogrammed?"

"The ones who work in the Wizard's office. But they're lying! I know he had planned to be gone just overnight on some secret errand for the Wizard. He wouldn't go and get himself deprogrammed without getting in touch with me . . . h-he loves me!"

Lettie drew in her breath, feeling a twinge of pity for this wretched child and fervently hoping that her own guess was wrong about what might be keeping Brian. "Please try to calm yourself. I need a description of your young man, his family's name and address, and a photo."

The girl loosened her grip on Lettie's neck and asked, "Why?" with a puzzled frown.

"So I can try to find Brian for you."

"You'd do that?"

"Of course. If I don't get anywhere with a few discreet inquiries, I'll give the police the information."

"I don't think Brian would like the police looking for him."

"I don't expect it will come to that."

The Druidess searched Lettie's sympathetic face, then said, "You sound like you know about these things. His name is Brian Albright. His father, Douglas, lives on Brampton Road." She removed a scrap of photo from the locket around her neck. "I'm afraid this is the only snap I have of him." It was a very blurry black-and-white picture of a bearded youth."

"That's quite a beard," Lettie remarked.

"Oh, it's not real—that's his Druid beard. Look." She pulled a wad of grey hair out of her smock pocket. "We must carry one of these at all times. It's a symbol of our faith."

"Could I have a closer look?" Lettie requested in a careful voice. The Druidess obediently handed it over. Lettie dumped it into the basin, turning on the faucet.

"What are you *doing?*" the girl cried shrilly. "That's no way to treat a symbol!"

Ignoring her protests, Lettie examined the sodden mess. Yes, it looked just the same! "You must trust me, dear. I want to help you. Now, what is the name of Brian's dentist?"

"His dentist?"

"You must trust me," the older woman reiterated.

The younger hesitated, but was finally persuaded by Lettie's guileless blue eyes to rely on this providential, if enigmatic, fairy godmother. "He uses the Heathrow Dental Clinic, as we all do. I don't know which dentist."

"Thank you. Now, chin up. I'll be in touch just as soon as there's word. . . . How silly of me, I don't know your name!"

"Cassandra Collins."

"How do you do. I'm Lettie Winterbottom. Call and leave a message with my housekeeper in St. Martin's Mere, if you hear from Brian, would you?" She squeezed Cassandra's hand. "Now I must go . . . oh, here's your beard back, I'm sure it'll dry out quickly."

Cassandra wiped the tears away with the damp beard and made gulping noises. Lettie flashed an encouraging smile and left the loo.

Outside in the hall the sales team was patiently waiting. They pressed a brochure into her hands, saying it was a financial statement detailing the company's net worth and growth potential. Not giving them a chance to launch into another spiel, Lettie lifted her chin and pronounced in regal tones, "Yes, yes! This is all most impressive. But I shan't place an order with anyone but your president, himself."

Alarmed glances darted between the three. "I'm afraid that the Wizard's schedule is very full just now. I'm certain that his personal assistant would be more than happy—"

"No!" Lettie stubbornly set her jaw. "I make it a policy to never do any business with a firm unless I've met the president."

After another fierce round of smarmy remonstrations, one Druid finally broke down, throwing up his hands and sulking over to a white phone hanging on the wall. He turned his back and mumbled into it for a while, listened, then turned

139

to her, holding the receiver slightly away from his mouth. "I'm so sorry, but the Wizard's personal secretary—"

"Tell the Wizard it's urgent that I speak with him about Brian Albright," Lettie insisted.

The name seemed to mean nothing to the salesman, but he repeated the message into the phone. There was a brief pause and he hung up, saying in a voice husky with amazement, "Please permit me to show you where the Wizard's offices are located, Miss Winterbottom."

The New Wizard was a large man with a very white complexion, red lips, and wavy black hair. He had a broad, pleasant face marred only by a prominent five o'clock shadow under his nose. He wore a pale grey suit, white shirt, and striped silver tie— everything correct and of good quality. When Lettie was shown in, his nearly seven-foot frame was stretched out on a long, green velour couch as he talked into a dictating machine. He put down the microphone and got to his feet, towering over her as he clasped her tiny hand in his.

"Charmed, Miss Winterbottom." He released her hand and indicated a choice of several brown corduroy chairs clustered casually around the divan. When Lettie was seated he said, "If you don't mind, I'll resume my prone position. Back trouble, you know—a common ailment among giants." He had a slight burr that made this remark sound like a line out of Robin Hood.

"I'm so sorry," she murmured.

"Aye, it is a nuisance to a man of my energy! But I don't let it get the better of me!"

"No, one mustn't do that."

As the Wizard lay down he returned her courteous smile. But he soon discarded it in favor of a more forthright expression of mild annoyance. "I have conflicting impressions of you, Miss Winterbottom. First you claimed to be a buyer who wouldn't put an order with anyone but me. When that ploy didn't work, you mentioned someone named Brian. Frankly, I'd like to know what it is you want."

"Stonehenge, Mr.—er—Wizard."

The man's dark eyes narrowed slightly. He took in a chestful of air and launched into an impassioned monologue. "Aye, this Stonehenge mystery has been a boon for sales. There's been a deluge of orders, from mugs to martini glasses. We are presently working overtime to turn out new models with 'Who Stole Stonehenge?' painted underneath the old decal. We've also got a short-sleeved 'Who Stole Stonehenge?' T-shirt in production, as well as an 'I Stole Stonehenge' long-sleeve. There's no doubt we'll make a packet before it's all over, but the rumours that my people are responsible for this blasphemous crime are too absurd to credit. But the rumours haven't hurt us! I estimate that twenty-eight percent of our increased sales on Stonehenge items are due to these libellous insinuations. For that reason, I have decided to let them pass without comment."

"And what about Brian Albright? Are you going to let him pass without comment?" she gravely inquired, fixing him with a penetrating stare.

The Wizard abstractedly massaged an area on his back just above his Gucci belt. A dangerous light appeared in his eyes. "What exactly are you implying?" It was a wary question. He'd just perceived this antique miniature for the elemental force that she actually was.

"Brian Albright was in Little Puddleton on your orders the night the stones were taken out to sea. He hasn't come back yet." The man's jaw slackened, exposing a row of teeth that wouldn't have looked out of place on a thoroughbred racehorse.

"There is no way you can prove that outrageous accusation!"

"There are such things as dental charts, Mr. Wizard."

"Aye, and there are such things as libel suits. Even if Brian Albright was there, you'll never prove it was on my orders."

"But it could implicate you," came her cool reply, in spite of the indignation boiling just below the surface. "The police may think he was one of your gang of burglars, who slipped, and fell to his death. Or worse—you could be tied into what may well be his murder. But not to worry—the publicity will sell plenty of T-shirts."

In the face of this threat, the Wizard rolled off the divan, landing on his hands and knees. He was temporarily reduced to emitting gobbling sounds, but gained control of his tongue as he gained his feet. "On my sainted mother's grave," he shouted, "I did not steal Stonehenge!"

"Perhaps not. I have a theory that Brian Albright might have been on the scene because you had reason to believe the stones were there. . . . You might not be the thief, but you have a very good idea who is."

At that inopportune moment, just as the giant

seemed about to crumble at her dainty feet, the door was thrown open and in dashed one of his lackeys, eyes wide in alarm as she shouted, "It's the Inland Revenue! They're confiscating everything!"

The Wizard's eyes bugged. "Of all the bally cheek!" He lunged towards his desk and wrenched off the head of the Druid doll that squatted by his phone. This peculiar action sent a wall of book shelves sliding open, through which the Wizard beat a fast retreat, bellowing an exit line in her direction.

Watching the panel slide closed again, Lettie pursed her lips in perplexity. What could he have meant? Was his last remark an admittance of guilt to income tax evasion—or piracy of ancient monuments?

Her deliberations were ended by shouts and running feet. There was panic among the Wizard's underlings. A distraught Druid burst through the door, looked around, and charged out again without seeming to have noticed Lettie standing by the desk. She sat down and dialled the *Plain Speaker* in Amesbury.

"Hullo. May I speak to Mr. Hilsebeck?"

"Who's calling please?"

"Lettie—"

"Ah!" The voice butt in, as if anxious to prevent her from giving her full name. "He's out of the office just now, but left a message that he would meet you at Tim's cottage."

"But . . . oh yes, of course. Thank you."

12

AN OVERJOYED TIM DANCED in circles, yapping a welcome to his mistress as she hung her coat in the hall cupboard and looked around with satisfaction. In the time she'd been gone the decorators had finished papering the hall. It had always been a dark little tunnel but the new pattern transformed it: green ivy and pink roses twining up white lattice created an attractive arbour effect. But Lettie noted with displeasure that the heavy mirror and dark walnut hat rack spoiled the illusion; something would have to be done about *that*.

Lettie passed through the living room, seeing that the painters had only one wall left to cover with that deliciously delicate peach; then she could hang the new slate blue and lavender curtains.

It was late afternoon. All the workmen had gone, as had the housekeeper, leaving poor little Tim on his own for hours. She scooped up the squirming terrier and let him lick her ear. In his enthusiasm he nibbled off her pearl earring, clamping his jaw shut over the prize. She had to scold and eventually pry his teeth apart, or he would surely have swallowed it.

She went into the kitchen and put the kettle on, sighing contentedly. She took her teacup into the living room and lay down on the chesterfield. Tim jumped up and curled into a black ball at her feet. In a few minutes she was asleep.

She woke to Tim's fierce bark and a persistent rapping at the front door. It took a moment to get her bearings and remember that she was expecting her sidekick. A peek through the curtain confirmed that he had indeed arrived.

"Come in, John David!"

"Hullo, ducks." He gave her shoulder an affectionate squeeze. "It seems like ages since we sat here and made our pact."

"So much can . . ."

"Can't it just? We've got a lot of catching up to do."

"Let me take your coat. Oh, look at that stain! Fortunately I have something utterly reliable that will take it right out. Would you like some tea? A piece of cake? No? Come into the living room, then. I have information that the police should have as soon as possible. I would have called it in myself, but thought better of it. It would require less explanation coming from you."

"Good job!" J.D. nodded admiringly, then collapsed into a chair.

She briefly described her escapades at the Iron Grove. He howled with laughter when he heard about the Most Enlightened One's other job. "What a headline! 'Dinky Dupes Druids,' with a subhead: 'Who Was That Masked Man?'"

"Of course you can't print a word of it. I gave him my assurances."

"All right," he groaned. "Go on."

She then told him about her visit to the New Grove, their ceremonial beards, and the missing Brian Albright. "Here, I jotted down his parents' address and the name of his dental clinic. The police ought to be able to compare his dental charts against. . ." She faded off, unable to bring herself to finish, the image of poor Cassandra was too sad.

"Too right. Where's your phone?" He gave the Amesbury police the tip and abruptly hung up, cursing. "They wanted to know where I am. . . . I've been followed, by the way, but probably not by the police. I had to abandon my motor and take the train over here to make certain I'd lost them."

"Isn't that a coincidence! Just as it looked like the Wizard might reveal all, the Inland Revenue men chased him away."

"You're certain they were the tax boys?" J.D. asked, abandoning his slouch for a more alert posture.

Lettie shrugged. "I wondered. I didn't actually see them. It's also coincidental that just before escaping he shouted over his shoulder at me, 'I've been shadowed!'"

"'I've been shadowed,' eh? It strikes me as too timely an exit." She said it was likely that someone had been keeping the New Grove under surveillance; a competitor, for example, or the real force behind the removal of Stonehenge. Her snooping might have triggered the whole scene. Agreeing that it was a possibility, J.D. continued, "Still, it's not so surprising if they were following him. He sounds like a damned fine suspect. He has the work force, maybe even the money, and the contacts to buy the expensive equipment. That's something I'll have to fill you in on."

"And then there's the incriminating beard. If it turns out that the corpse is indeed Brian Albright, one of his tribe . . ."

"And he openly admits he's growing rich on the souvenirs—a pretty convincing motive for the crime." The clock ticked away a few minutes before J.D. continued. "I now have a good idea what device was used to move the stones. It's called an airlift. Just one costs a cool hundred and fifty thousand pounds. They'd have needed as many as a dozen. Does the Wizard have that kind of kale?"

By way of an answer, Lettie produced the financial statement that the Druid sales team had given her. Opening it out on the coffee table, they scanned the statistics together.

"Unless these figures are queer, it looks like the Wizard's doing all right for himself; but he doesn't have the cash or credit required to buy a fleet of airlifts. He's got enough on his plate just paying for his extravagant new building."

"Could one rent airlifts?" Lettie asked.

"No, I checked on that."

"I see. That seems to weaken the Wizard as a prime suspect," she said with some regret. "Now tell me about your investigations."

"They're not as colourful as yours," he began, "but at last I think I've got a clear idea of the mechanics of the job. I believe we are correct in assuming that the crew came up river by boat, with at least a dozen men to take their equipment up to the site via airlifts, pull the stones down, and literally float them on air down to the river. I expect that

147

their original plan was to try and take them down river straight off. But the storm was too much of a hazard and there was no hope of getting out to sea at that time. The canal must have been an alternate plan."

"Well, at last we know something of the method!" She gave him an encouraging smile that soon grew a bit thin. "Still. . ."

"I know," he said with a weary shake of his head. He reached for a cigarette, remembered it was against house rules, so he nibbled on his knuckles instead. He got the idea from Tim, who'd been noisily chewing on his tail for the past hour. "It still leaves a tremendous amount of legwork. I have the name of the company who exclusively distributes the airlifts. I even got the names of the members of the board. Haven't yet had the time to find out if they're loose-lipped with their customer's names, but I don't expect they will be."

"Is there any chance that you've noticed any suspicious names among the board of directors?"

"That would be too much to hope for. It's the sort of research that could take weeks to follow up."

"And we don't have that much time. I think the most direct course to take would be down river. Let's see if we can find anybody who noticed our boatload of scoundrels."

"That's what I was about to suggest," he said. "But we ought to rent a boat—that's the best way to explore the river. Meanwhile we'll have to use your car and I'll try to stay out of sight. A quasi-governmental company called JETCO has got someone on my tail."

The ringing phone prevented further explanations. Lettie went into the hall to answer it. "Julia dear!" he heard her chirp. "I got home just a few hours ago . . . how silly of you to worry."

He closed his eyes and sifted through the events of the past week, trying to separate the chaff from the grain. He kept puzzling over that aerial photo at Nordstromson's. The enlargement clearly showed the circle of radar vans with their antennae aimed straight up. That didn't seem right. He was certain that radar pointed out, not up. Did this somehow connect with the code name "Operation Red Blinder?" He was beginning to formulate a theory when Lettie came back into the room.

"Julia got Nordstromson's paper translated. It's Swedish. And we were right about its content—the standard anti-nuclear arguments."

"I see. For some reason I'm losing interest in Nordstromson." He yawned.

"Dear me, it's getting late!" his hostess exclaimed, glancing up at the mantel clock. "I'll go put linens on the guest room bed."

"Do you mind if we watch the news before we adjourn for the evening? It's a professional habit. I can't sleep not knowing whether or not I have to get up early to cover the dropping of the Big Bomb."

Lettie leaned over and turned on the telly. The blank tube filled with the BBC's familiar talking head as the sound came on in the middle of the report. Hilsebeck, nodding off after a time, jerked back to consciousness as he heard his name.

". . . Hilsebeck, the Amesbury reporter who has covered the disappearance from its initial discovery, is wanted by the CID to assist with their inquiries. Edward Jenks, Hilsebeck's editor at the *Plain Speaker*, said that neither he nor the reporter were available for comment at this time."

"Poor me," J.D. groaned, inverting Beerbohm's quip about Oscar Wilde: "I woke up famous and go to bed infamous!"

13

"WE'LL BE IN AMESBURY in a few minutes," Lettie
called over her shoulder to her partner, who'd
spent most of the journey from St. Martin's lying
out of sight on the back seat. It was a posture inspired by fear of her driving style, as much as
dread of being apprehended by the police, or whoever else was now officially after him. As they
slowed in dense traffic he pulled the lap rug over
his face. It itched and smelled of terrier, contributing a little more to his discomfort. The prospect of
even a few more minutes in this erratically careen-
ing vehicle made the drizzle outside seem attractive.

With a resounding thump as Lettie cut across a
parking curb, the vintage Humber swayed to a halt.
She alighted, looked around, then tapped an all-
clear on the rear window. He got out and she un-
locked the trunk for him, holding an umbrella over
his head as he struggled into a heavy yellow oilskin
and matching hat. "All I need is an eye patch to
look a proper old man of the sea," he muttered.
"Let's hope nobody recognises the notorious reporter skulking around under thirty pounds of
yellow vinyl."

As they crossed the puddle-choked car park to the boat rental shack, they reviewed their cover story. Lettie was to be a researcher and conservationist of river wildlife. Hilsebeck was her loyal, taciturn boatman. Such was their excuse for being out in a rented boat in weather patently inappropriate for just a pleasure excursion.

The rental hut was a decrepit affair manned by an ill-humoured adolescent, intermittently munching the contents of a bag of crisps and braying along with the distinctly antisocial lyrics goose-stepping from his radio. He didn't even spare them a second glance as he counted their money twice, then carelessly tossed a set of keys marked "Fortuna" in their general direction. They left him to continue contentedly drumming and snarling away at Western Civilization as he knew it.

Little more than a pier and car park, the rental operation only managed to survive because of its proximity to the traffic bridge. The roar of the motorway filtered across the water as they glumly eyed the *Fortuna*. She was a twenty-footer with faded blue paint, her interior awash with oil-rainbowed bilgewater that sloshed around as the boat rocked. J.D. slid back the hatch that opened down into the narrow cabin; one glance at the dark coffin, vile with the smell of fish oil and kapok, was enough. He closed the hatch and said to Lettie, "You'd better sit on the wooden cover over the engine. Here, this cushion should make it more tolerable." In this way they were both under the sagging canvas awning and out of the wet.

Surprisingly, the engine caught immediately, settling into a muted burble. "This should be child's play," he sang out, engaging reverse and opening up the throttle, which got them a full three feet up river before they recoiled forwards. Lettie, trying to keep her boots above the foul wash, nearly toppled backwards. The pilot smiled sheepishly, then went to undo the bowline. "Yo ho ho," he called out with a little less conviction, trying again—this time with more caution.

Once they were out into the centre of the river, there was little to do but steer, the current providing all the impetus they needed; the engine purred along good-naturedly. The banks of the river were mostly bordered by fallow farmland and small houses. The *Fortuna* came upon only a few larger docksides. It soon became apparent, even to their landlubber eyes, that genuine shelters from the storm were few and far between. In the rare cases of dangerous weather, most of the local craft were small enough to be pulled on shore or stowed away in boathouses: or so they were told at the little marinas they investigated that provided fuel, bait, ice, and gossip. Any one of them would have taken note of a large vessel making a major purchase of fuel or supplies at this time of year. But as the *Fortuna* neared the river mouth, the detectives had not found anyone who'd serviced or noticed any remarkable sort of craft.

"They made at least four trips this way; you'd think somebody would have spotted them en route," J.D. grumbled as they walked away from a bait shack a few miles north of Christchurch. "Even if they passed by in the wee hours! I thought boat people always got up before dawn to poop the

153

decks, or whatever it is they do." He put out a hand and helped her back onto their rocking craft.

"Somebody must have seen them. We just haven't been fortunate enough."

He shouted above the putter of the engine: "I can only conclude that this tub isn't very well named—unless it's for tuna."

They continued their journey to the sea. The only protected harbor they found was at Christchurch, with its small sheltered roadstead directly off the rivermouth. Here was home port for a modest fleet of yachts, trawlers, and coastal lugs that sailed the Solent.

It was afternoon as they tied the *Fortuna* up at the fuel pier, admiring a nearby pleasure cruiser that made their shabby craft look particularly sad. As they were lashing down their mooring lines in a mess of knots that would have made a Sea Scout blush, a fat woman with a baby face came out and cast a dubious eye on their boat. Leaning against the pump, she looked imposing in what appeared to be a water resistant pup tent and a crumpled canvas hat, shiny with glued-on fish scales. "How much fuel?" she asked in remarkably cultured, musical tones.

"Top it, if you please," he said, without a clue where the tank was located, or how much it held.

She sniffed once, then turned the pump selection to diesel fuel. In a matter of seconds she had the fuel cap off and the noxious smelling oil gurgling in. "Chesterton and Cole?" she asked, one boot up on the gunwale. When her customers looked blank, she patted the engine cover affectionately. "A courageous engine, in its day." She swept her soft,

154

bovine eyes across the unkempt decks of the *Fortuna,* then settled on J.D.'s new yellow kit gleaming in the wet. "Spiffy gear." She grinned.

"Pooles and Cundey," he replied. "It's what anyone of quality is wearing this season."

She made a gurgling sound at his joke. Lettie inquired if she was the proprietress of the establishment. "Yes, it's my shop," she replied, shutting off the pump and screwing in the cap. "That will be three pounds forty."

They followed her into a commodious and orderly store. There were racks of nautical gear that made J.D.'s kit look too chichi for words. Across the aisle two weather-beaten types were discussing the comparative merits of nets. "Sheila," one said, "I think you've made a sale—if you can put it on account."

"I'll do that, Jack," Sheila said, then turned her attention to making out a chit for the fuel. The reporter read the logo on the top of the pad: WILLIAM CHANDLER.

"Are you Mrs. Chandler?" He asked.

"Not any more," came her blasé response. "Care to open an account?"

"That's very accomodating. Is that your common practise?"

"I do a fair amount of billing." She slipped out of her tent and hung it on a hook where it dripped musically into the bucket below. She smoothed down the broadest expanse of fisherman's sweater J.D. had ever seen. He caught Lettie looking at it too; no doubt calculating how many skeins of wool it represented. "And I've had very few troublesome accounts."

155

"Ah well, I suppose I ought to just pay cash."

As Hilsebeck produced a roll of notes and began counting them out, Lettie asked for advice, explaining, "We're trying to ascertain if it's possible to maintain a year round barge on the Avon in order to do riverine research on waterfowl habitat."

"An occasional barge does go up this time of year. I serviced one just last week."

"Is that right? How big was it?"

"A large seagoing number, very shipshape. For its size it's perfect for upriver; you could float it through the reeds and not leave a bent rush. Wonderfully roomy living quarters to stern, and quite a good-sized hold."

"It sounds like you went on board?" Lettie asked hopefully.

"No, I'm just reminiscing. My uncle owned a similar barge when I was a child. I used to skip rope in the hold."

"I see. Do you suppose a vessel that size could get through the ice that was blocking the river until a few days ago? I would need to get through—even in weather like the recent storm. Constant research, you know," Lettie added.

Sheila wrinkled her snub nose. "Let's see . . . after they bought fuel, I noticed them heading for the river. It was early evening, but I can't be certain about the date."

"The storm lasted from the tenth until the thirteenth. The river was frozen until the sixteenth," J.D. said, then had an idea. "Do you have a record of the sale? That would tell us if they took on the river ice."

"It would be so helpful!" Lettie smiled persuasively. "I must research this sort of thing before I can authorize spending our society's funds on such a major project."

The shopkeeper obligingly thumbed through her file of the month's transactions. "Here it is," she said, waving a receipt, which the reporter neatly plucked from her fingers.

"Ah, that was January sixteenth," he nonchalantly remarked, memorizing the other salient facts, which were salient indeed. "There you are, thanks very much." He returned the bit of paper with his most engaging smile.

"You've been most kind!" Lettie exclaimed. "That seems to indicate that they went upriver after the ice had begun to melt. I suppose we must next interview barge owners about their experiences with winter conditions." She tugged at J.D.'s arm, saying, "It's getting late."

As they fumbled with the lines Lettie demanded to know what was on the sales receipt. After a moment of teasing, he finally told her. "We're in luck, my good woman! It was a charge. To be billed to the Institute for Innovative Celtic Studies, Kilterry, Ireland."

As her whistling pilot steered for the river mouth, Lettie threw open her arms and emitted a series of delighted chirps into the wind. "Maybe it's only wishful thinking, but I can't shake this sudden delicious feeling that we're about to win the Irish Sweepstakes!"

"We are, my darling dewlap, we are! All we have to do is locate our lottery ticket and collect the prize—a small matter that shouldn't require more than another day or two of swanning about in elegant yachts, just one step ahead of the police."

14

THE INSTITUTE for Innovative Celtic Studies didn't appear in the Index of British Institutes at the Salisbury Public Library. Lettie replaced the thick volume on the reference shelf, and suggested that they check the periodical file for a magazine or monthly newsletter.

They located the Periodical Index amid dictionaries and abstracts in a corner under a stained-glass window near the study tables. "Ah!" J.D. exclaimed a bit too loudly, as his finger came to a stop beside The Journal of Innovative Celtic Studies. Several orderly young children in maroon school blazers glared at him as they looked up from their work.

"I'll go request back issues," Lettie whispered and crossed the alcove to the periodical desk, returning with a stack of magazines. She gave him half, and they bent their heads to earnest research. He first jotted down the address for subscription requests, which corresponded to the one he'd obtained from the charge slip in Christchurch: Postal Box 43, Kilterry, Kildare, Republic of Ireland. After reading several articles, Lettie looked up frowning. "This isn't quite the scholarly magazine it pretends to be."

"How so?"

"No scientist worth his sheepskin would make such free interpretation of the archaeological evidence. Now take this outlandish essay on pre-bronze burial middens by someone named Ben Shatto—" She gasped and clutched at her heart.

"What is it? Are you ill?"

"Aye, Ben Shatto," she croaked, staring off into space. Just as he was about to run out of patience, she emerged from her catatonia. Her face radiant, she gripped his arm and poured a stream of breathless words into his ear. "Remember my interview with the Wizard? I had just insinuated that he might know who was behind the theft. . ."

"Yes, go on!"

"Before he could reply the Inland Revenue supposedly sent him in full retreat. On his way out the door the Wizard shouted what I understood to be 'I've been shadowed!' That, of course, was my error," she said with a finality that implied everything was now perfectly explained.

"An error about what?"

"Don't you see? He wasn't shouting 'I've been shadowed' at all; he was actually answering my previous remark—telling me who he thought stole Stonehenge!"

There was a long pause before the penny dropped. "'Aye, Ben Shatto!' instead of 'I've been shadowed!'" J.D.'s eyes bugged and his jaw fell slack with amazement.

"That's it. A heavenly clue, isn't it? It reminds one of the pivotal clue in MacDonald's great classic, *The List of Adrian Messenger*—and it's the very inspiration I need to start work on a new novel!" The faraway look was returning.

Leaving her to it, he went out to the call box in the lobby and phoned the morgue at the *Plain Speaker*, requesting a file search on Ben Shatto and the Institute for Innovative Celtic Studies. The search would require a few minutes, so he hung up and stepped outside for a smoke. As he lit up he noticed that his hands were shaking. He could almost smell the fox just ahead cutting through the thicket.

Pacing in front of the library's notice board, he thought about the leader of the New Grove. It was useless to surmise how the Wizard had caught on to Shatto, but he'd obviously had his suspicions early on, since he sent his own Druid spy down to Little Puddleton. What had the Wizard intended to do? Nab Stonehenge and expose the thief? What a publicity coup that would have been! But the Wizard had been neatly put to flight before he could make his next move. Had Shatto been behind the attempted bust? If so, his intelligence system was very good indeed.

He looked at his watch and dialled the morgue. "Hilsebeck here. Find anything?"

To his surprise, it was Jenks himself on the other end of the line. "Just heard you'd called, laddie; thought I'd tell you personally that the cops are after you."

"So I've heard. Do we have anything on Ben Shatto?"

"This Shatto is an elusive devil," the editor drawled. "A powerful figure in the military-industrial complex who spends a packet to keep his name out of the papers. His hermitage is somewhere in Ireland; we couldn't find out where. As for the Institute, it's a queer bunch—their only public activity seems to be putting out a quarterly magazine stuffed with raving Celtomania."

"Who's the head?"

"All we've got is a pseudonym—doing business as."

J.D. had his pen poised. "Let me have it."

"Merlin the Younger," Jenks said with a perceptible sneer.

"As in Camelot?" J.D. asked incredulously.

"Right the first time. Found a flak sheet our Merlin sent round, trying to get a write-up in the books section. He traces his lineage back to the original magician. Fascinating, eh?"

"Anything in that flyer I can use?"

"Not unless you're in need of something to spread on your roses, but I'll read it to you."

Hilsebeck listened to the recital, then said, "I'll be in touch tomorrow. And lay in a few magnums of bubbly; I think I've got my man."

"Look lively, or you'll find yourself in the nick. The gendarmes are beating the bushes for you. They're leaving 'No Stone Unturned.' Like it?"

"Love it, great headline," J.D. growled and hung up.

Back at the table where Lettie was poring over the magazine, he dragged a chair out with a harsh sound that brought heads up all over the library. The librarian frowned and lifted a finger to her lips. J.D. rolled his eyes and sat down. "Find anything else?"

"Yes, there's been an article by Shatto in every

161

issue since the magazine first appeared three years ago. No other writer contributes on such a regular basis." He then repeated what he'd just learned from Jenks; her eyes widened as she absorbed this. "Merlin the Younger! One of the oldest legends about Stonehenge is that each stone is a petrified giant that Merlin magically transported from the Plains of Kildare to Salisbury Plain."

"Kildare . . . the institute's mailing address is in County Kildare."

A glance at a map of Ireland revealed that the Plains of Kildare were located just southwest of Dublin. The River Liffey flowed fairly close to the village of Kilterry, then another forty miles to the sea at Dublin.

"We're going to Kilterry!" he declared as they beamed at each other, confident that the prize was once again within their grasp. But their elation was short-lived. Outside there was the grinding of brakes; boots clumped up the steps as a dozen soldiers stamped into the library. Lettie was instantly out of her chair and out of sight behind a tall shelf of encyclopedias. J.D. sat transfixed, a doomed rabbit fascinated by the closing hounds.

"May I help you, gentlemen?" the librarian inquired.

"No, thank you," one of the soldiers replied. His eyes searched the room and rested on Hilsebeck. A quick cock of his head in the direction of their quarry, and they all advanced.

"Not to worry, I'll go to Kilterry. Follow my trail, if you can," came Lettie's whisper from the other side of the shelf behind his head.

He didn't answer; he was too busy cursing.

The librarian and well-mannered children looked on as the army escorted him out the door. "And that's what can happen if you have rude manners," a bespectacled, pigtailed youngster smugly remarked to her classmates.

As they shoved him into the back of the truck, J.D. noticed a slope shouldered figure smoking a black cigarette. He was in whispered conference with an army officer.

As the green coastline of Eire loomed out of the fog blanketing the entirety of Saint George's Channel, Lettie was glad she had opted for the Swansea Ferry rather than a direct flight to Dublin. Standing out here in the tangy salt air was so much more pleasant than the recirculated fumes and cramped seats of an airliner. And they would have charged her an extra seat for Tim, a practise blatantly designed to discourage a little dog's custom. Here on the boat he not only had the run of the decks, but was spoiled by the predominantly Irish crew. Whoever had described the Irish as lovers of music, horses, and dogs had not been far off.

Upon disembarking, Lettie took the shuttle into Cork, getting out at the downtown terminus. She was booked on the express coach to Dublin, which would pass quite near the tiny village of Kilterry. In a last flurry of packages, coats, and umbrellas, the passengers found their seats. It was a noisier, jollier crowd than one encountered on an English bus. Several passionate conversations from the rear revolved around the football pools; nearer at hand there was a general discussion about the foolhardiness of the plans to construct a new dam on the site of an old fairy fort. "The wee folk will be taking the water, sure."

The miles passed quickly as their omnibus skirted the flanks of County Cork's Knockmealdown Mountains, then over the modestly proportioned Galtees into the heart of Tipperary and the Golden Vale. Being an express, the bus's only scheduled stop before Dublin was at the crossroads town of Port Laoise. When the driver announced the stop Lettie went forwards and asked him where she could catch a local bus to Kilterry. The driver would have none of this. The village lay just off Route 7, and he'd be glad to pull over and let her walk the short distance, if her baggage wasn't too heavy. She thanked him, pleased that the word express was so flexible in Ireland.

When Lettie alighted, the driver and several passengers gave her a wave. She and Tim were glad of the opportunity for some exercise. It was a quiet afternoon, gently drizzly; what the Irish call a "soft day."

Lettie was, as usual, well-equipped. Her handbag was stuffed with nibbles for herself and Tim, and she carried several rolls of linen that would be put to use later, if all went well. In addition, she'd brought a copy of her favourite walking guide, which had a good deal of information on Kildare. She stopped next to an old stone roadmarker and consulted her foldout map of the county. It would be an ideal site to hide Stonehenge! It was lightly populated, and there was plentiful access, either from the River Liffey that wound its way down to Dublin, or from one of the spurs of the Grand Canal that bisected the Republic from Dublin in the east to Galway on the western coast. The guide mentioned a few of the great estates, but it would take a local's knowledge to direct her to her goal.

The village of Kilterry was extremely small, little more than a handful of what had once been workers' houses grouped around a sleepy crossroads. The post office was an adjunct of the grocery store. There was also a church and a pub. She entered the latter; the dark, stale-smelling room was empty except for a man behind the bar counting his bottles.

"I beg your pardon," she said to a narrow bent back in a red plaid shirt.

"No need, dear lady!" He swung around to face her, a cigarette hanging from his lip. He was a dried up old codger with a hoarse voice and bad teeth. "Any break from this bloody inventory is welcome. The Myth of Sisyphus, it puts me in mind of. You know the one—every morning poor old Sisyphus is after rolling the big stone up the hill until he's bleeding at the knees. Every evening it rolls back down again."

"It's never been a favourite of mine."

"Small wonder, it's not a very amusing way to spend your time, is it? But sure it's better than having a raven eating at your liver. I'd rather bleed at the knees than have anyone monkey with my liver. Excepting myself!" He let out a laugh that evolved into a violent coughing fit. Resolving to avoid telling him jokes, for fear of doing him in, she averted her eyes until the hacking began to subside. He took another deep drag on his cigarette, which brought on another brief spell. "Is it a nip you're after?" he was eventually able to ask.

"Not exactly. I was hoping to get directions to the Shatto estate. I understand it's very near here."

"Sweet crippled Jesus!" the barman exclaimed, then clamped his jaw shut, a shrewd look in his eye.

"I'd be happy to pay something for the information," Lettie said, after an uncomfortable silence.

But the offer seemed to give offense. "Bollocks! I don't pull my forelock for anybody!" came his quixotic pronouncement, followed by a cackle that launched him into another paroxysm of coughing. Lettie made a quick exit; she had no wish to cause him further harm.

The street was empty except for a woman on a bicycle, who readily pointed eastward, saying that Shatto's estate was only a short walk. Lettie passed a shabby farm before coming to a high stone wall. It extended for most of a mile down the lane, all done in the local style of flat stones fitted together and chinked with grass. It was a beautiful wall spoiled by the No Trespassing signs and tangle of concertina wire along the top. Even the heavy gate gave her no view as she ambled past; the wrought iron had been backed with sheets of black metal.

She took a rest on a tree stump at the point where the wall turned a corner and stretched away from the road, hugging the soft contours of the terrain. It presented a formidable barrier as far as her eye could see. Tim yapped and pulled at his lead, so she unsnapped the leash and let him run. He set off to explore, dashing a few yards into the bracken and disappearing. When she could no longer hear the growls that characterized Tim the Explorer, she got up and set off after him.

It was easy to locate his escape route; a small

stream meandered through a low grated opening in the wall. The stream was concealed from the road by the hollow it had eroded. On the other side of the grate, which resembled a medieval portcullis, her black Scottie romped in forbidden meadows. The grate was altogether too small for an average sized adult; but it looked like a petite size might just squeeze through.

The first attempt was hampered by her coat and hat. She removed both and hung them on the iron crossbars. After an awkward moment of danger to both dignity and apparel, she was through with only a few splashes above her waterproof boots. Apparently Shatto's isolated grounds hadn't been exposed to the skillful maraudings of children, or he would have closed up the hole more thoroughly.

She strode across the meadow, Tim's wagging stub of a tail a beacon as he ran on ahead. They crossed several acres of empty pastureland and once at the top of a series of gentle rises Lettie paused, careful not to silhouette herself against the skyline.

The stream could just be seen curving beneath a cluster of ancient yews. On the far hill a splendidly proportioned grey stone house stood surrounded by fallow gardens and an extensive park, all circumscribed by a circular drive. High shrubs screened the main buildings, which included a garage and a stable.

She was about to reach for her miniature field glasses to study the house when her eye was caught by an architectural anomaly: a great smooth curve, as pure as an enormous billiard ball, just clearing the tops of the trees. At first she mistook it for a neoclassic dome, but her glasses revealed no surface detail. It looked more like the top of a weather balloon.

She removed the strips of cloth from her purse and rolled them out on the protected side of the hill, securing with rocks the simple message for J.D., should he fly over. In the event that he arrived by land, the barman would at least remember Lettie's request for directions to the Shatto lands. She could only hope that her partner was not far behind.

With Tim at her side, she went into the woods, moving as quickly and quietly as possible. A startled pheasant exploded from a thicket, while a jay looked unperturbedly down from a fir branch. She was unaware of another eye that was watching—a dead, unwavering orb.

Hilesebeck's cell had all the amenities: a WC without a door or seat, a cot stuffed with something mouldy and lumpy, and a rust-stained basin that continually backed up, flooding the perpetually dank concrete floor. In the Guide Gulag, these accomodations would rate no better than two bent forks. The naked bulb, glaring from behind its steel mesh, completed the superior atmosphere. Stripped of his watch, he had lost all sense of time. Sleep deprivation, disorientation, isolation—all by the book. No obvious harassment, just the cold empty minutes that melted together, blurring away the hours and even days. They were softening him up.

He sat on the edge of his pallet, trying to gauge time by the stubble on his jaw. He knew he could hold out for quite a while longer—but what about Lettie? She had been very much on his mind; he was afraid she would be needing him. He had to get out of this cell, and could think of only one potential key—Operation Red Blinder. He had spent his jail time working things out. It wouldn't be easy to lie to the interrogators that he would have to face. His only hope was that his best guess was some small part of the truth.

If only he had some idea how long he'd had been here! Timing was critical—he mustn't fold too soon, or they might get suspicious. Doubtless their manuals contained a chart predicting just when a lazy, uncooperative Aussie should crack. But if he waited too long, Lettie could be in jeopardy. He wished for the thousandth time that he could just sneak a look at a calendar.

15

AT FIRST LETTIE WAS UNCERTAIN how she would
cross the stream. The distance to the other side
was less than a yard, but it was deep enough to
preclude wading. Tim sniffed at the edge of the
bubbling water and concurred. A short distance
downstream was a single-arched bridge constructed
of field stone; it was, however, too exposed for her
to use. As far as she could see, this was the only
crossing for motorized traffic. It was interesting
that the bridge had not been considered strong
enough; a new concrete pylon rose out of the
shaded water to support the center of the span. To
her own eye the bridge appeared in excellent
shape, with the substantive look of a structure that
could support a delivery van. Had it been specially
reinforced for a heavier load? On the order of fifty
tons a lorry?

Eventually, she found a tree trunk that spanned
the water a bit further upstream and made an ade-
quate, though shaky, footbridge. When she reached
the edge of the woods the white dome was just a
few yards beyond. Like a silk bubble the size of several tennis courts, it filled an open area that had

been recently bulldozed out of the forest. The earth was still raw and artificially flat. A heap of tree stumps had been pushed into a burning pile. The muddy, track-marked ground was stacked with enough construction materials for a large project— from the look of things, a permanent addition to the estate. She could just discern the purr of an electric motor, accompanied by the gentle sound of rushing air. It came from an insulated box whose thick, flexible umbilical hose was hooked up to the fabric bubble. It must be a tent, Lettie decided, supported by the air pressure built up by a fan. The inside would be unobstructed, with room enough for virtually anything, but it was only a temporary structure. She had once attended a dog show at Chichester where all of the judging had been inside a similar, though smaller, tent.

Heart in throat, she took a quick look round before approaching the bubble. She was more than a little frightened, but the conviction that Stonehenge was just ahead drove her onwards. Tim ran ahead, dashing off behind a tall stack of lumber. There was a startled yelp, unlike his normal glass-shattering cry of discovery. Lettie hurried around the end of the obstruction, and nearly ran head-on into a sinister figure clad in a dark paramilitary uniform. He carried an automatic rifle and clutched Tim against his chest. Lettie froze, worried that Tim might be in danger. She found this sudden dark apparition alarming, but was determined to keep her wits about her. "Ah yes, Mr. Shatto is having me to tea. Could you direct me?" She hoped this rough-looking fellow wasn't some sort of IRA soldier. What a pity it would be if she'd found the wrong address.

"I'll talk! I'll talk!" Hilsebeck produced a convincing sob as he beat his tin food tray against the cell door. The racket was merely for show; his playpen was undoubtedly wired for sound. He found kicking up a fuss amusing, a welcome change from lounging around and looking mopey.

Presently a blank-faced guard opened the door, and a phalanx of troopers escorted him down the hall into what could only be the interrogation room. A weedy young soldier switched on a tape machine as J.D., trying to look the beaten man, folded into a hard wooden chair. Around the table was assembled a mixed bag of military and civilian personnel, among them none other than Colonel Bellows. Now that the head of Salisbury's military contingent was here, the big guns could be brought to bear.

"Mornin' Hilsebeck," Bellows said in a carefully neutral tone, although his eyes shouted, "Traitor!" Further down the table a civilian sighed and examined the ceiling. "Cigarette?" Bellows offered, enjoying the role of Grand Inquisitor and savouring the thought that the time had come for revenge.

The prisoner humoured him by smiling weakly, accepting one from the proferred pack and looking around for a light. Bellows nearly threw his shoulder out leaning towards him with a lighter. J.D. sucked in a lungful of smoke. "I'm prepared to make a statement."

Bellows smiled smugly."Very well." For a long moment the room was nearly silent; then a chair creaked and one of the military aides cleared his throat. Bellows sat back, his moustache drooping on his blouse front and his chins folding in on themselves. "Just let it flow, Hilsebeck."

J.D. quietly announced that he wasn't going to tell them anything until his conditions were met. Eyebrows were raised, but Bellows seemed unperturbed. "You are not in a position to negotiate. Why, under the Official Secrets Act alone—"

"I assure you I'm up on the subject, Colonel." The prisoner swallowed nervously, then carried on. "That's why I've got to have your guarantee that I won't get the ax." Reactions to this consisted of an exchanged glance or two and general shuffling of papers. "I don't sing without protection against harm from your side"—he looked up and down the assembly—"or theirs."

"Theirs?" Bellows couldn't quite disguise the triumph in his voice. "You are referring to your Russian superiors?"

"Precisely. Who was Red Blinder meant to blind, eh?" J.D. tapped his cigarette out on the table top for emphasis, as the room collectively tensed at the mention of the operation. The reporter continued to remain dull-eyed, to cover the fact that his mind was cracking at top speed.

"Very well. I am authorized to grant you immunity from prejudicial treatment. Carry on," Bellows commanded.

"In writing."

"Em?"

"I want it in writing, on HM's stationery. And duly witnessed."

Bellows's face momentarily clouded over. He

shot a silent question at a dour civilian, who nodded almost imperceptibly. "All right," the colonel said. "It will take a few minutes to type. But I hope you aren't stupid enough even to consider trying to waste our time!"

"Of course not," J.D. said innocently.

J.D. folded the document and began to recite. "For some time there have been rumours among the citizenry that secret weapons are being tested at Salisbury. But things have been busier lately, haven't they, Colonel? And our organization of diabolically clever pinko spies put the pieces together from satellite pictures, intercepted messages, and the like. I frankly don't know exactly how your security was breached; that wasn't my department."

"Was there an inside source?"

"I doubt it, but I can't be certain. My mission was to cruise around, ear to the bush telegraph. There were some interesting occurrences, you must admit—all those defunct tellies and wirelesses in the area, not to mention the strange lights in the sky. And the timing was curiously right: just when a big storm grounded all air traffic and snarled local communications. An optimum time to try a few modern war techniques; that was the Blinder part, wasn't it? In some way you boys artificially generated the type of electromagnetic phenomena that would accompany a thermonuclear blast. Just like a decent sized nuke can produce a ball of hot plasma that would interfere with radar, satellite relays, etcetera. Ergo the Blinder part of your operational code name—shamefully easy clue, that." J.D. retreated back into his chair as he studied their reactions to his bold guesswork and bald-faced claim of spying. To his gratification, no one spoke for quite some time: several of them even looked shaken beneath their professional veneer. His guesses must have been spot on.

The interrogation was finally over. Bellows and a couple of MPs escorted Hilsebeck down the hall leading past the detention block. But instead of returning him to his cell, they shoved him into a room that was occupied by Nordstromson and a uniformed man who was staring out of the barred window. The MPs were told to stand guard outside. "You've got your five minutes," Bellows directed at the uniformed back, then withdrew, locking the door behind him.

Gunnar Nordstromson was sitting forwards on a grey metal service chair, elbows on his knees in an uncharacteristically humble posture. He nodded at the reporter, then resumed gazing at the numerous heel marks indenting the worn linoleum.

"I've been worrying about where you'd gotten to, Nordstromson," J.D. said. "Nice to see you looking so well. I've been wondering all sorts of things about you lately. Like why your references don't check out."

"That must have been the army's doing." The Swede's tone was weary. "They wouldn't want the press getting anything on the spy until they'd made up their minds what they wanted to do with him."

"I see. I bet you've been having the deuce of a time explaining away those classified maps you've got. It made even me a little suspicious."

This remark brought the officer around to stare

175

at J.D. with a mixture of disapproval and embarrassment. "It was my fault that Gunnar—er—gained unauthorized access to that material," he declared in a voice and accent identical to the archaeologist's. There was even a slight facial resemblance.

"This is my brother, Commander Stefan Nordstromson," Gunnar said, then matter-of-factly added, "I stole the map from him."

A few more pieces fell into place. A foreign officer of rank in the middle of a host nation's intelligence network. "So Red Blinder is a joint operation, eh? You must be military liaison. Or are you in charge of the Swedish part of the job?"

The older Nordstromson looked disgruntled, and his brother reassured him. "Don't worry, he's only a clever guesser. He's no more a Red spy than I am. An ignorant, unscrupulous yellow journalist, and fortune hunter, nothing more."

"Thanks for the character reference, old chum. Now tell me how you managed to convince Bellows you aren't a Commie. I could use some pointers."

The situation obviously pained the civilian much less than the military man, who was quick to explain. "We proved to Bellows that my brother's enthusiasm is based on a certain naïveté. . . ."

"It's hard to be naïve about nuclear weapons these days," J.D. interjected. "One stumbles over them everywhere." The remark brought a glint to Gunnar's eye, who might not be as cowed as he was endeavouring to appear.

"Enough. Your opinions don't interest me," the commander said with a hardening of his long jaw.

"What does interest me is who implicated my brother."

"So *that's* why you arranged this meeting." But J.D. was still puzzled. "Why didn't you just ask Bellows who it was?"

"For his own reasons he cannot personally tell me." With a glance around the room that made it clear the walls had ears, he added, "I am sure he has good reason."

"Well," J.D. said after a moment's thought. "I see no reason not to speak my mind. My vote's in for a reporter named Devereux who works for the *London Daily Journal,* and it seems he's branching out. He could have called the cops, but after seeing what was on your desk, I think he got the inspiration to cut a deal with the army. In a good faith gesture, he threw me in as a bonus."

"Or to eliminate competition in the Stonehenge Sweepstakes," Gunnar suggested.

"But that didn't work," J.D. said as they heard the key turning in the lock. He leaned forwards and in his best Bogart imitation whispered, "I'm breakin' out a dis joint, see? I gotta deadline ta meet."

"A deadline with destiny," the archaeologist said with a comic flourish. J.D. laughed regretfully. He had trouble completely disliking anyone with a sense of humour.

"Good afternoon, Mr. Shatto. My name is Lettie Winterbottom." She smiled, rising from the chair she'd nervously waited in for hours, the well-behaved Tim lying at her feet.

Ben Shatto was every inch the country squire,

ramrod straight in his shooting jacket and cap, which he now carelessly dropped onto an exquisite rose-coloured Victorian love seat. His yellow-grey hair was parted in the middle and combed back at the sides, his clipped moustache was vintage Anthony Eden. He had a narrow face with dark blue eyes so large and round that they overpowered the rest of his face. Distinguished, accustomed to power and prerogative, he looked like a true gentleman of the old school.

"Pleasure," he said after laboriously clearing his throat.

"I do hope you'll forgive this intrusion," she murmured.

He took a chair on the other side of an inlaid Louis XIV card table that Lettie had been admiring. The two-tiered room, which apparently served as both library and conservatory, would have been intimidatingly echoey if it hadn't been for the clutter of furniture. There were a dozen Hepplewhite chairs crowded around a fine old campaign desk ruggedly out of proportion with the delicate pieces surrounding it. The desk and shelves of leather-bound volumes behind it looked well-used. The antiques were crammed together randomly, dictated by the eye of a collector, not a decorator.

As he stared out the French doors at the park, he once again made a rumbling noise in his throat; she assumed it was either a nervous mannerism or a sign of some health problem. "Your intrusion, as you call it, is most welcome, Miss Winterbottom," he said in a conversational tone. "It indicates that my fortress is not as secure as I'd imagined. I've sent for tea; I hope that will be suitable?"

"Perfectly."

"You must have a touch of a chill from tramping about outside."

The tea came on an elaborate old Sheffield silver service, delivered by a proper butler, instead of the rifle-toting bodyguard that she'd expected. Shatto poured, and they politely chatted about antiques. Shatto's enthusiasms were solely in things past. His attitude towards modern artifacts was obviously indifferent. Yet she knew he was a powerful industrialist who had made his fortune manufacturing modern military hardware. But he was also the writer of the mystical claptrap in his Celtic review. Here was a curious amalgam indeed.

She set down her teacup, feeding a last crumb of bun to Tim. "You've been a gracious host, but I'm afraid the time has come to be painfully direct."

"Very well. I must confess a certain amount of curiosity concerning your presence, not that it isn't a respite from my usual companions —my staff. I have no family, they died in the War."

"What you call your staff, I'd call your henchmen!" she remarked, remembering the half-dozen muscle-bound brutes who had surrounded her outside and escorted her into this room. She knew that two had been standing guard outside the door ever since.

Shatto looked mildly amused. "Henchmen, if you like. It has a rather piratical dash."

"And you, sir, are the pirate."

He considered this a moment, all the while producing his low growls. The sound was beginning to unnerve Lettie, and made Tim cock his head and stare up at the man, as if expecting a bulldog to

179

emerge suddenly from his waistcoat. "Tell me, Miss Winterbottom, what brought you to my fortress?"

"An almost imperceptible trail. You've been very clever."

"And what trail might that be?"

"Unmarked snow . . . ice swept away in the fog, a corpse, a journal of letters. Not to mention the occasional unforeseen obstacle that came our way," she added matter-of-factly, wondering how J.D. was faring against the most recent hurdle.

"*Our* way?"

"Yes. There are others involved, of course." They regarded each other intensely now, all polite circumlocution forgotten. They had maintained a cool front, but his was beginning to waver, giving her a startling glimpse of the obsessed creature behind those remarkable eyes.

When he spoke the troublesome hoarseness had overtaken his speech. "Then there shall be more desecration! I've fought all my life to keep out the madding crowd, and now you're bringing them down upon me!" These last words were uttered in an almost incomprehensible croak. His fists were clenched at his side.

She remained calm, aware that to betray any fear might prove her undoing. "On the contrary, you've brought them on yourself. It was foolhardy to assume you could get away with stealing Stonehenge and not have the outside world come after you."

"Steal!" he cried incredulously. "I did not steal it! I reclaimed it from the clutches of the Philistines! How could I turn my back on the spray-paint on the holy stones? How could I allow those ignorant savages within a hundred miles of my. . ." He was unable to continue as his eyes filled with tears.

"I understand," she gently replied.

"I assure you the man's death was accidental. We didn't even know he was there, only heard his last. . ." His face paled, the stress of the last few weeks showing plainly. "We were having any number of control problems. One caisson wasn't properly inflated, and the poor bastard had the misfortune to be in the wrong place at the wrong time. . . . I don't even know who he was."

"His name was Brian Albright," she said, although she didn't know this with absolute certainty; it seemed best to sound in possession of all the facts. "He was sent by the leader of the New Grove to investigate. The Wizard was on to you, of course. Is that why you had the Inland Revenue set upon him?"

He blinked in amazement, then recovered a remnant of aplomb. "Apparently I waited too long to get him out of the way. Pulling the right strings in the government took more time than it should have."

"How did the Wizard get the scent? And how did you become aware of how close he was getting?"

"Two years ago I made a very discreet attempt to buy the land Stonehenge stood upon. I was determined to get the stones out of the public sector and safely back into private hands. You see, I've never had any faith in the government's ability to protect them permanently. When the Wizard somehow heard about my attempt he was very much against me. He was afraid that if Stonehenge was no longer open to the public, his souvenir business would suffer; so he went to a great deal of trouble to get a spy into my organisation. I was instantly aware of it, of course; my security system is the most sophisticated in the world," he admitted with pride, then added with a paranoid's conviction, "It has to be!"

"And what did you do about this spy in your midst?"

"I kept him. It was a simple matter to monitor what information he was fed. I did, however, transfer him to an assignment in Germany when I planned the Stonehenge extradition, so he wouldn't get wind of it. I have a factory there; I sent him to help secure it against espionage. But, I suppose as soon as Stonehenge was reported missing and the Wizard heard that his man had been sent out of the country, he became suspicious. I should have prepared for that eventuality. It was a regrettable oversight."

"How did you hope to prevent the Wizard from catching on?"

"It was overly optimistic, I must now admit. But I was counting on the odd phenomena that Red Blinder created to distract him and everyone else. He couldn't have known what to make of it."

She was at a loss to know what to make of it herself, but tried to look knowledgeable. He gave her a rueful sideways glance, wondering too late if she knew about Red Blinder. Ever since the electronic eyes had picked up this unlikely trespasser, he'd been gripped by a befuddling disquiet. During tea with this elfin lady, his ears had filled with the terrible roar of flood waters smashing through his walls and sweeping away his precious stones from the

Golden Age—the Golden Age he had, for a few days, repossessed.

His worst fears were realised. There was a sharp knock at the door, and his head guard entered. "Sorry to barge in, sir, but our instruments have picked up helicopters approaching. They will be coming in over our southern walls in a matter of minutes."

A tight smile on his lips, Shatto gave a mock bow towards Lettie, the instrument of his misfortune, then motioned his man out onto the balcony for a quick conference.

The sound of rotors was growing louder as Lettie craned her neck to scan the sky. She squelched an impulse to jump up and run over to the window; it wouldn't do to rub it in. It really was too bad; she was sorry for the blow losing Stonehenge would be to Shatto. At the same time she was very much relieved. She hadn't had time to work out a detailed plan of escape, in the eventuality that J.D. might not manage to get out of jail and come to her rescue. She wasn't surprised that he'd come through, but she hadn't expected him to bring so many friends along.

16

HILSEBECK HAD TO WONDER at it all. He had managed, without getting into too many specifics, to raise quite a bit of excitement. Red Blinder was obviously hot stuff; it had taken less than two hours to mount what was really an invasion force, although nobody was calling it that. Bellows was flushed with battle fever as he paraded up and down the drafty, vibrating hull of the big helicopter. It had been too many years since the old boy had enjoyed any action.

Only the journalist seemed to be worried that they were violating the sovereign air space of the Republic of Ireland with three army helicopters packed to the portholes with soldiers. Bellows apparently considered Red Blinder worth immediate action and expected to get in and out without being caught. J.D.'s mind was boggling—it was difficult to believe that these SAS commandos would soon be descending on the quiet land below. Bellows paused beside the prisoner, bending down to shout above the ear-splitting thwack of the blades. "Coming up on the coordinates now, Hilsebeck. Earn your keep!" J.D. followed the colonel forwards to the flight compartment. Through the clear perspex nosepiece the deserted village crossroads were clearly visible.

Never having set eyes on this countryside before, J.D. hadn't the foggiest idea where to look for Shatto's estate. "Don't recognise it from the air, I'm afraid," he yelled.

Bellows tapped him on the shoulder with his swagger stick. "Let's not have any of *that,* m'boy. We can't hang up here all day. Sooner or later, they'll start chucking potatoes at us."

"Circle around to the east," J.D. directed the pilot. "Then swing out in a concentric search pattern." They swept around the village, widening their distance from this centre point as Hilsebeck scanned the unpopulated countryside for clues. There would have to be a road wide enough for flatbed lorries, since the nearest waterway was several miles away. Privacy would be another prerequisite; a large estate with high walls would be the ticket. He didn't expect to see the monument standing out in the open; a protective structure would be more likely. A couple of large barns, at least. He was beginning to sweat when the pilot banked them sharply around, calling, "We've got a marker down in that pasture!"

J.D. looked past the high wall, catching sight of his own initials spelled out in white streamers. Lettie, bless her, thought of everything!

"Take a look at that dome," the pilot shouted out of one side of a concerned frown. "Rockets?"

"No, just communications," J.D. ad-libbed, smiling widely as he regarded what looked like just another of those radar domes that dotted many a modern landscape.

"Damned cheek!" Bellows rumbled, leaning over J.D. for a better view. "Right out in the open like that! Leave it to the bloody Irish!" Celtophobia was obviously an important part of Bellows' makeup. "Back in your seat, Hilsebeck, I've got the helm."

With the aid of his radio headset, Bellows directed the other two helicopters, dividing them into separate assault groups that landed on either side of the mansion. In the weak light that filtered through the scudding rain clouds J.D. could just see the troopers running out of the craft and taking up positions behind privet hedges and fountains. Bellows leaned forwards and yelled something into the pilot's ear, while pointing down at the clearing around the mysterious bubble. Although unable to hear over the roar of the engines, J.D. had no trouble interpreting the pilot's curt shake of the head: there was not enough room to set down their big ship in so confined a space. J.D.'s own eye confirmed the pilot's judgment.

So it took him by surprise when he felt the elevator stomach that went with rapid descent; they were spiralling down into the tight clearing. Hilsebeck braced himself; this was no autumn leaf, but twenty tons of metal and explosive fuel. Within moments the topmost boughs of the trees were above his porthole.

They stopped their descent just a few feet from the ground. There was a strong smell of hot oil from overheating gearboxes as the ship strained to hold position. Bellows pointed at Hilsebeck, and two troopers frogmarched the reporter to the back of the ship. He got a quick look out through the open ramp before being catapulted into space.

The mud should have felt soft, but his flapping overcoat had gotten tangled in his legs, and he hadn't been able to avoid coming down hard on his back. He lay still, fighting for air while commandos landed on every side. Above him the oil-stained belly of the helicopter gleamed in the reflected glow of its landing lights. For a ghastly moment it seemed to be falling towards him, then lifted up and away. The two men who had chucked him out reappeared and helped him to his feet as he coughed air into his lungs. He was very shaky and caked with mud and debris the helicopter had blown around.

Bellows deployed his skirmishers around the perimeter of the clearing, then collared J.D. "Move!"

J.D. gazed at the dome looming in front of them. Not much doubt what was inside! It was imperative that he go in first—there was no way he was going to let a quarter of a million dollars go to some corporal as discoverer. Or worse, Bellows! Time for subtlety. "Rank has its privileges, Colonel." He waved the officer ahead.

"Not bloody likely!" Bellows snorted. "You are going in first and having a little disarming chat with any comrades that may be about. Cover him." The two guards obediently cocked their submachine guns as Hilsebeck, trying to look reluctant, headed for the modest little door set in the curved wall of the dome. "We'll wait outside for two minutes," Bellows warned. "Bring any occupants out, or we'll let the air out of this bag the quick way."

J.D. opened the door and stepped into the first

chamber, a closet-sized wooden construction serving as a crude air lock. Another door lay just ahead. Outside, his army escorts closed the door behind him as he approached the second. He put his hand on the lever and pulled slowly. There was a sigh of wind as it opened.

Inside a soft pearlescent glow created an eerie, almost undersea effect. The distant sound of air blowers muted any sense of the outside. The famous stones rose magnificently before him, arranged in the familiar horseshoes, the heavy lintels laid across their supports. He stepped through one of the arches, standing at the center of the circle. Even in this alien setting, Stonehenge radiated its own aura of time, a compelling mystery in a world that had long lost the key to its secrets. Laughing softly, J.D. ran his fingers along the lines ancient tools had made, and was surprised at his own emotion. It really wasn't just the elevating thought of the loot, or the gratification of winning.

He was groping for the words to pin on the experience of Stonehenge itself, when a voice said, "Hands above the head and don't move." J.D. obeyed as a gun barrel poked into his back. There was a crackle of automatic weapons fire outside and some incomprehensible shouting. J.D. stood very still, afraid to turn or ask questions while the firing went on.

But the silence that followed seemed even more ominous. What sort of hornets' nest had he stirred up? Could it be that Bellows and his men were now also at the uncomfortable end of the gun?

"I hope you're all quite comfortable." Shatto's voice

reflected the victor's control of the situation. "Your men are being looked after on the lawn, Bellows. Any casualties requiring medical attention?"

"Not to my knowledge," the losing side mumbled.

There were two armed guards at the door. Lettie and J.D. made up the rest of the party. They had managed only a few quick words during their recent hurried reunion after the battle.

Bellows' personal troops had been surprised in the open by a superior force. Fatalities would have been inevitable if the defenders had not immediately opened up with a barrage of tear gas accompanied by rapid bursts of fire over the SAS troopers' heads.

Bellows, who knew quite well who Shatto was, spent several unhappy moments being cursed by the lord of the manor. From the moment Shatto identified himself, the colonel knew that he'd been caught up a gum tree. Hilscbeck refrained from comment. Judging from his colour, the colonel was well beyond seeing the macabre humour of the situation.

Now a sulky Bellows sat across the room from J.D., bitterly plotting his revenge against the lying scum who had promised him Red spies, and had gotten him in Dutch with an important name in the military hardware business instead.

"The cover of darkness should allow you to continue on your way." Shatto was standing in front of his fireplace and smirking at the glum colonel. "I take it you didn't find the time to clear your arrival with Irish authorities? I thought not. I'm certain they will understand that mechanical problems brought you down on the way to Belfast. I will, of course, verify this. I have some influence locally."

J.D. chose that moment to break in on what had been a one-sided conversation. "I've a few questions that require answers."

"I don't believe any explanations are owed," Shatto said stiffly. "Considering the provocative nature of your own actions, you would be wise to leave well enough alone."

"I can't do that," came J.D.'s reply in his best stubborn manner. "So, who were the lads following me in the grey Cortina?"

"I have no idea," Shatto replied, settling into his leather commander's chair. With the conqueror now seated, the vanquished officer took his turn pacing in front of the fireplace, keeping one eye on the newspaperman, who was obviously bent on stirring up even more trouble.

"You ought to," J.D. countered. "They had a JETCO sticker on the bumper. For employees—your employees."

"That may be so, I couldn't say. I sit on many boards besides JETCO's."

J.D. chewed on his moustache while deciding if there was any harm in airing a few conclusions. It was now or never. "They could have been your boys—or else Intelligence men working undercover at JETCO trying to find out what you were up to."

Shatto looked sideways at Bellows and commented that such operations were common enough. "I might do the same myself, given the proper circumstances. It isn't unheard of in a firm that manufactures military equipment," he said offhandedly, dismissing the suggestion.

J.D. shook his head. "That won't wash. I'll tell you what I think happened. Bellows' SAS patrol at Stonehenge took down my Volvo's registration number when Lettie left it parked at the scene."

She nodded but remained quiet in her corner. It was entertaining to watch J.D. in action; his clarity of expression belied his thoroughly disreputable appearance.

"The SAS checked me out," the newsman continued, "and put a tail on me around the time of my interview with Captain Tree. And I now understand what was behind it—your involvement with Operation Red Blinder. Knowing when it would take place must have helped your Stonehenge plot enormously. The weather conditions would be ideal, and communications fragmented. Not to mention the strange phenomena Red Blinder produced. All of it adds up now! Red Blinder would require the most advanced electronics, manufactured by your companies, and guarded by Bellows. That would neatly explain why the Cortina with your employee sticker was after me. They were working with the SAS. Care to comment on any of this?" He turned from Shatto to the colonel, who only stared coldly back, the picture of cornered bloodymindedness.

Shatto said, "It's only a theory. It doesn't deserve serious thought."

"Fortunately it really doesn't matter," J.D. said. "There's a solution to our dilemma."

"Solution? What solution?" the colonel blustered derisively, but nonetheless orbited in closer to the reporter's chair.

191

"I propose a mutual defense pact," J.D. said. "Each of us wants something, after all."

Bellows pointed an accusing finger. "You want to get your grubby mitts on the reward."

"Correct. Lettie and I want the reward for finding Stonehenge. You, Colonel, wish to avoid this blot on your copy book; letting a reporter suck you in about deadly pinkos is bad enough. And if Shatto's caper comes out, it will make your intelligence network look like a sieve. He nicked Stonehenge right under your nose and used your secret operation to cover the crime. I'm afraid that publicity about all this could be fatal to your career. Of course, Shatto wouldn't be at all happy about it getting out either."

"You are proposing a cover-up?" Shatto asked.

J.D. nodded. "The two of you should be quite adept at skullduggery. It wouldn't be the first truth you've suppressed."

"Then that is what we shall do. Only I see no need to return Stonehenge; that can be our little secret, eh, Colonel?"

"You'd have to dispose of both of us, you know," Lettie said quietly.

"And the stones as well," J.D. chimed in. The tension in the room was increasing markedly.

"I'm afraid I don't follow you." Shatto was beginning to look annoyed, an indication that he followed very well.

J.D. removed the kid gloves. "Come off it! You've been off your nut thinking you could pull this stunt in the first place! What chance have you got now when the local authorities will be checking out reports of gunfire and helicopters landing? Questions will be asked. A word or two will leak out. Once the first crack in the dike appears, you'll need an army of Little Dutch Boys."

Bellows muttered that they could take Stonehenge out to sea and sink it, for all he cared, a remark that earned him a steely look from the thief, who declared emotionally that he couldn't bear to part with the stones.

"Spare us the martyred tones! You bloody well can! We can all make the required sacrifices. I, for one, will take myself off this story, rather than be part of publishing the phony stuff you'll be concocting. In fact, I will voluntarily leave the country. But you will have to give up the stones. A theft has been committed against the British people, a crucial point that you can't continue to ignore."

Hilsebeck could feel the tables turning. There seemed to be hope when Shatto admitted in a hoarse voice, "This proposal has some merit . . . but the treatment of the stones—"

"That's the beauty of it. What better way to publicize the frailty of the monument—and the neglect it has received? In crude terms, Stonehenge is now box office. When it is returned, security will be tightened up considerably," J.D. pointed out reasonably.

"Perhaps," Shatto reluctantly conceded.

"Good," J.D. said briskly. "Now there's another issue. Lettie, my dear, I can't ask you to go along with this morally reprehensible solution unless you can accept the necessity of it."

"You'd jolly well better hear *my* opinion—" Bellows' outburst was nipped in the bud by Shatto ges-

193

turing towards his guards. The colonel was wise enough to bite back any further remarks.

A pool of light from a Tiffany lamp illuminated her gentle, fine-boned old face under a halo of silvery curls. Lettie looked from one tense face to the next and sighed regretfully. "It's a clever plan, John David—so worldly and diplomatic. It certainly would be worthwhile to try to avoid the awkwardness between the governments of England and Ireland that would inevitably arise, should word of this incident get out. But we cannot forget that a man died while Mr. Shatto was engaging in his activities. Unfortunately we have only his word for it that the death was accidental. We are obliged to see that he stands trial."

"They'll never prove it was murder!" Shatto croaked from behind the hand that now propped up his forehead, obscuring his eyes.

J.D. had to agree. "I was the only bystander, and I couldn't see what actually happened. It will be Shatto and his crew's claim that it was an accident, against whatever scientific evidence the police can muster to the contrary. Chances are there won't be enough of that to prove murder."

Lettie nodded. "That's quite possible. Still, these days police science is capable of producing truly remarkable evidence. And it might all be in Mr. Shatto's favour, who can say? The crux of the matter is that we have no right to interfere with the due process of our legal system."

"You're absolutely right, but the fact remains that such interference happens all the time." Her partner shrugged.

"Surely while you were growing up you heard a

mother's response to that argument—just because others do it, doesn't make it right." Her delivery was quiet, but they could see that she was in dead earnest.

"So be it," Hilsebeck muttered, looking properly chastened.

"I'm terribly sorry, Mr. Shatto," she said, sadly regarding the perfect part on his bent head. "I suggest that you offer to return the stones immediately; that might make the court go easier on you."

To her amazement, this kindly advice did not produce the mollifying effect she'd intended. Shatto flashed a defiant look at his tormenters. "Never!" he shouted. "Do you understand? Never!" He was on his feet, strutting before them, rallying the mental defenses that had seemed completely beaten only a moment before. "Just run along now, all of you. And be thankful I'm letting you go! If you dare even start a rumour about what has transpired here, I shall guarantee you your international incident! And don't think the Irish government won't back me up! They will refuse to extradite me or the stones. You didn't pull a fair cop, you see— Bellows here commited an illegal act of aggression on foreign soil."

"Oh gawd!" J.D. groaned.

Shatto snapped his fingers at his guards. "Our guests are leaving now. Round them all up and see to it no one is left behind." Then Shatto stalked out of the room, without so much as a pleased-to-have-met-you.

195

17

IT WAS A FEW MONTHS AFTERWARDS, in late spring, that Julia visited her aunt in St. Martin's Mere. The two women were lounging on a wicker swing among the lilacs admiring Lettie's expensive new, oversized Victorian-style gazebo, while Tim rolled on the grass in the foreground.

"I'll plant wisteria, of course. And tulips, primroses, and perhaps a pink azalea," Lettie bubbled. "By next year, if I fertilize liberally, the plants might be mature enough to warrant a photo story in *Famous British Gardens.*"

Julia shook her head in mild exasperation. The *Sunday Supplement* article featuring the interior of Lettie's cottage apparently hadn't been enough. "Now Auntie! Gwenna Hardcastle has fifty acres of park with a maze, a dozen fountains, and a hundred ghastly examples of Baroque garden statuary. You haven't a hope of outdoing her with your quarter-acre of garden. Isn't it enough that you are at last as famous as she is, with your picture in every newspaper in the world for finding Stonehenge? Promise me you'll forget this absurd rivalry with a dreadful old snob you've never even met!"

"Julia, what *are* you going on about?" Lettie asked, her face set in the stubborn lines of incomprehension that always appeared whenever Julia mentioned the natural enemy.

"Have it your way," the younger one grumbled.

"Speaking of Stonehenge," Lettie brightened, reaching into the pocket of her new jonquil yellow garden smock and pulling out a handful of clippings. "Wouldn't it be fun to make a scrapbook of the case? You're so artistic, I thought you might organise the stories and help me get them pasted into this book."

"That sounds like a genteel pastime for two ladies on a spring afternoon," Julia agreed, and began arranging the clippings in chronological order. "The aftermath seemed to drag on forever, didn't it? It was a news editor's dream."

"Look at this, J.D.'s exclusive: 'Crazed Celt Cops 'Henge.'" That was the story that broke the case wide open. Before it was all over it had cost Bellows his career and Shatto thousands of pounds on extra guards and equipment to keep the hoards of journalists and gawkers from getting over his walls.

The Irish government, at first overwhelmed by events, responded with patriotic fervor to news that England had invaded their soil. Irish honour was further insulted by Whitehall's initial refusal to confirm or deny that Stonehenge was there. It had taken Hilsebeck's story, naming Shatto as the thief, to force the first grudging apologies from HM's government.

"I must say, I still think Ireland's indignation was more than justified," Lettie declared as she reread an article from a Dublin paper describing their government's response to England's requesting the stones' return in exchange for clemency to Shatto. REPUBLIC STANDS FIRM: NO TO ENGLAND. A famous Irish-American columnist phrased it in more vulgar terms: MICKS NIX FIX.

Meanwhile Shatto's public relations staff were doing their utmost to portray him as a modern martyr to the Black and Tans. Shatto shrewdly applied for asylum for both himself and Stonehenge on the grounds of religious freedom.

This clever ploy stalled negotiations until a bright Ministry legal counsel found the key: both countries were signatories to international agreements regarding criminal activity. One of the conditions of these treaties was that evidence found in one country could not be withheld from another. The counsel pointed out that the stones themselves were not just peripheral evidence, but the actual weapons used in what might have been murder.

DOLMENS OF DEATH the headlines screamed, this time with no lyrical accompaniment from Hilsebeck's pen. He was too busy trying to force the American newspaper to fork over the reward money. He finally did obtain assurances that the cash would be forthcoming once the stones were standing again on Salisbury Plain.

England's Prime Minister eventually made a public apology and Ireland arranged for the return of the stones. Shatto was extradited into custody of the CID, but never stood trial. A preliminary inquest found Brian Albright's demise to be death by misadventure. Shatto pleaded guilty to grand theft. The court fined him fifty thousand pounds and required that he undergo psychiatric treatment.

There were the usual protests of preferential treatment for a rich man with close government ties.

"Just looking at this snapshot, I can see that he suffered for his mistakes." Lettie frowned sympathetically over a photo of a haggard Shatto being escorted from his hearing. "He certainly aged after that fateful afternoon we had tea."

"These are my favourites." Julia held up the full-page photo coverage of the reward ceremony held at Stonehenge. The famous stones loomed impressively in the background as Lettie and J.D. gratefully accepted their honorary Druid beards from the New Wizard, while the Prince of Wales and other luminaries looked on.

"I *like* this picture," Julia said, smoothing out a photo of J.D. kissing Lettie's check as she daintily held up an oversized check with the maker's name large enough to read even on the murky newsprint. "And here's the supporting cast!" Julia pursed her lips critically. "I look like I'm already four sheets to the wind, the way Gunnar is holding me steady." It was a candid shot including Jenks and a brittle Devereux holding up their glasses in a toast to the triumphant detectives. Nordstromson had been forced to leave the party early to catch his flight to Stockholm. For reasons not publicly revealed, the Swede's work visa had been invalidated.

"There's just one more item to paste in," Lettie said. "A postcard from John David. It came yesterday. He's renting a luxurious beach villa in Bermuda and wants us to come visit while he waits out his citizenship. See, he underlines that you're invited too, dear."

Julia made noncommittal sounds and stooped

down to toss the stick that Tim had eagerly dropped on her sandal.

"Well, *I* may accept his invitation," Lettie admitted. "I've been thinking it might be time to branch out from writing just mysteries. The UFO books sell famously, you know. I understand that the Bermuda Triangle is practically a guarantee of a fifth printing, at least."

"If you go and solve the Bermuda Triangle, I shall never speak to you again," Julia said with a grin.